DAVE
and the
farting dog

Jim Eldridge

Illustrated by Jonny Ford

Hodder
Children's
Books

A division of Hachette Children's Books

Also by Jim Eldridge:

Disgusting Dave and the Flesh-eating Maggots
Disgusting Dave and the Bucketful of Vomit

To Lynne, now and for ever

A Catalogue record for this book is available from the British Library

ISBN 978 0 340 98157 3
Printed and bound by CPI Group (UK) Ltd, Croydon, CR0 4YY

The paper and board used in this paperback by Hodder Children's Books are natural recyclable products made from wood grown in sustainable forests. The manufacturing processes conform to the environmental regulations of the country of origin.

Hodder Children's Books
A division of Hachette Children's Books
338 Euston Road, London NW1 3BH

An Hachette UK company
www.hachette.co.uk

CHAPTER 1

'DAVE! STOP PICKING YOUR NOSE!'

That was my mum.

'John,' she said to my dad, 'tell him.'

Dad had just walked through the door, home from work. He looked at Mum, puzzled, and then at me, and then back at Mum again.

'Tell him what?' he asked.

'To stop picking his nose.'

Dad groaned. 'Not again! Dave ….'

'But it's part of Science,' I protested. I held out my finger so he could see the interesting black and purple crusty bits on the end of it that had come out of my nostril.

'Yuk!' said Mum, putting on her 'I'm-going-to-throw-up' face. 'Clean that muck off your finger at once!'

'OK,' I said. I put the end of my finger into my mouth and licked off the crusty bits with my tongue.

'Yeurghhh!' said Dad.

'WITH A TISSUE!' roared Mum.

'I haven't got a tissue,' I said. Then I remembered. 'Well, actually I do have, but I'm keeping a lump of snot in it so I can examine it under my microscope.'

FACTOID:
Snot
Snot is very important: it stops muck getting into our lungs.
When someone sneezes, snot belts out of their nose at 160km an hour!

That was too much for Mum. She left the kitchen and headed for the living room.

Dad shook his head. 'This has got to stop, Dave,' he said.

'But it's Science!' I protested. 'It's Biology! We do it at school so it must be all right.'

'Dave,' said Dad firmly, 'we are going to have a

serious talk about this later. Now go to your room.'

With that he left to find Mum and cheer her up.

Sighing, I headed upstairs to my room. As I got to the landing I could feel my intestines give a little churn and I let out some gas.

'MUM! DAVE'S FARTING AGAIN!'

This time the shout was from my dreadful sister, Krystal. She is thirteen years old and the most terrifying person on the planet. I made a run for my room to escape, but I didn't get there.

CRASH! Krystal banged the door open and stood framed in her doorway, glaring at me.

'You are disgusting!' she said. 'You are the most disgusting thing in the whole world, and that includes all the creepy crawlies and sludge and muck and everything that is revolting and disgusting! I hate the fact that you are my brother! In fact I'm not even sure if you are my brother! I think you were dumped on this family by aliens from the Planet Disgusting! What are you doing, farting outside my room?'

'I was going to my room,' I said, and held out the

rolled-up tissue to prove it. 'I'm going to examine some snot under my microscope.'

'YUK!!!!' And Krystal's face really curled up, her eyes going squidgy and her teeth sticking together. I saw her hand reach for a tennis racket just inside the door and I ran to my room and rushed in and put a chair against the door just in time. The tennis racket smashed against my door.

Like I say, Krystal is the most terrifying person I know. Even more terrifying than Banger Bates's dad who's in my class at school. Banger Bates, that is, who's in my class, not his dad. Banger Bates is the same age as me, eleven. His dad's much older, but if he was at school he'd be in the Reception class because he's an idiot. He's got tattoos all over himself and a big ring through his nose and he terrifies everyone at school, including the teachers. But even Banger Bates's dad isn't as terrifying as my sister.

I got out my microscope and was just putting a blob of snot on one of the slides when there was a knock at my door. It was too quiet and gentle to be my sister. When she wants to come in she doesn't knock, she just kicks down the door. Not that she ever comes right in, because she says my room's a Health Hazard. What Krystal does is stand in my doorway and shout at me when I've done something to upset her, like fart in front of one of her friends. This quiet knocking meant it was either Mum or Dad.

'Dave?'

It was Dad.

I moved the chair away from the door and opened it and Dad came in. He looked gloomy. I imagined he and Mum had just 'had words' about me downstairs. This usually means Mum complaining about me and Dad agreeing and Mum saying, 'Then why don't you do something about him?'

FACTOID:
Snot

Snot is mucus in your nose that hasn't got much water in it. The mucus collects the things you breathe through your nostrils: dust, smoke, dirt, pollen. When snot dries, it becomes bogies.

'Dave,' said Dad, 'we have to do something.'

He sat down on my chair, right on top of the piece of tissue with the rest of the snot in it.

'Er …' I began, thinking it a good idea to warn him what he'd just sat on, but I didn't get the chance.

Dad gave a heavy sigh. 'Dave, you are upsetting your mum and me with the things you do.'

'What things?'

'The disgusting things. Picking your nose and eating it. It's got to stop. Now we've tried talking to you about it. We've tried reasoning with you. There's only one thing left.' And he opened his hand and produced a twenty-pound note. 'Bribery.'

'Bribery?' I echoed.

Dad nodded. 'If you can stop doing anything disgusting for just one week – seven days – then I will give you this twenty-pound note.'

Twenty pounds! All for me! It seemed too good to be true. I looked at the twenty-pound note in Dad's hand, then at Dad, then back at the twenty-pound note. This all seemed too easy.

There had to be a catch.

'What's the catch?' I asked.

Dad shook his head. 'No catch,' he said. 'Just don't do or say anything over the next week that either your mum or Krystal or I consider to be disgusting.'

I thought this over. 'When you say disgusting …?' I began, just wanting to make sure of the rules.

'You know what I mean,' said Dad. 'No disgusting smells. No disgusting noises. No disgusting actions. And if you can keep it up for just seven days …' He rustled the twenty-pound note at me.

Twenty pounds! What I could do with twenty pounds! I could buy things for my microscope!

I nodded. 'Agreed,' I said. I held out my hand for the note, but Dad had twitched it away and put it back in his pocket.

'In seven days' time,' he said. 'Providing nothing disgusting happens.'

With that he got up and headed for the door.

'When does it start?' I asked.

'From now,' said Dad.

I gave him an awkward look. 'Actually, can we start it from about two minutes' time?'

Dad looked at me, puzzled. 'Why?'

'Because you've got a tissue stuck with snot to the bottom of your trousers,' I said.

Dad looked round at his bottom and his face did that thing when he goes silently, 'Yuk'. He pulled the tissue off the seat of his trousers and went to throw it in my wastebin, but it stuck to his thumb. He gave me a look that told me he wasn't pleased.

'I didn't know we were starting when I put it on the chair,' I said, trying to appeal to his sense of fair play.

Dad looked at the snotty tissue stuck to his thumb as if he were about to say something. Then he must have thought about a whole seven days of peace and quiet without Mum and Krystal complaining about me.

He nodded. 'The seven days starts in two minutes, as soon as I've got rid of this yukky thing.'

With that he headed for the door again. As he opened it, I belched. Dad turned and glared at me.

'Two minutes,' I reminded him. 'That's the last one.'

'It had better be,' he said. 'Or no twenty pounds.'

He left, shutting the door. I looked at my clock. I still had thirty seconds left, but I was taking no chances. I let out a silent fart, one last good one before I became a disgust-free zone for seven days.

CHAPTER 2

The next morning, I was really good at breakfast. I didn't make any windy noises, or examine the breakfast cereal in case any insects had managed to get inside the packet and die.

(I once spotted a dried beetle in Krystal's muesli and pointed it out to her just as she was about to put it in her mouth. After Mum had stopped Krystal screaming, she told me off and insisted what I'd seen was actually a raisin. I proved I was right by picking the dried beetle off the wall – where it had stuck when Krystal threw her spoon while she was having hysterics – and broke it in half to show them the dried-up insides of the beetle. Krystal then screamed so loudly she broke a lightbulb, and I got told off again – just for being right!

Life can be very unfair.)

I then set off for school, and – just in case I was being watched by any of the neighbours who might squeal on me to Dad and Mum – I deliberately avoided examining any of the dog poo on the pavement on my way there.

By the time I'd reached the school gates, I was feeling pretty happy about being well on my way to getting my hands on that twenty pounds, but then someone grabbed me by the collar and pushed me against a wall, and my feelings of happiness disappeared. Even though I'd been grabbed from behind, two things told me the person who'd grabbed me was Banger Bates, our school bully.

One was the size of the fist I could see out of the corner of my eye. Like Banger Bates, this fist was HUGE! And Banger Bates is ENORMOUS. I don't believe he is eleven years old, I think he is really about fifteen and his parents got his birth certificate mixed up with someone else's. Possibly a baby gorilla.

The other thing that gave him away was the smell. Banger Bates splashes on his dad's aftershave, even though he doesn't shave. This aftershave is like some horrible gas that brings tears to the eyes of anyone who smells it. Anyone, that is, except Banger Bates and his family. This stuff is so awful that if you splashed any near an animal you'd be arrested for cruelty.

FACTOID:
Bad Smells
The skunk is an expert at making really bad smells. It squirts a stinking liquid from glands under its tail up to a distance of three metres. The bad smell can be smelt up to half a kilometre away!

'So!' snarled Banger, and he spun me round so he could glare into my face. Banger does the glaring thing very well: his lips curl up and his eyes bore into you like a dentist's drills. He is terrifying.

I didn't say anything because I've found that if

you say anything to Banger before he's ready for you to say it, he's likely to bash you round the head and snarl, 'Shut up, creep!' or something similar. He glared at me a bit longer, as if he was trying to work out the order of his next words. (Banger is VERY thick, with about one brain cell inside his skull. But it's a very dangerous brain cell, because all it can think of is bashing people up.)

'So!' snarled Banger again. When I still didn't say anything, he added, 'Dickens!' which is my surname. Then he said, 'You're gonna look after a dog.'

I was puzzled. A dog? I looked around, but there was no sign of one. 'What dog?' I asked.

'My gran's dog,' said Banger. And then, as if he'd just remembered he was Tough and a Bully, he pushed his face closer to mine and growled, 'Or else!' in a menacing manner.

With that, he let go of my collar and nodded to me. 'Come and get it after school.' And he walked off, in through the school gates.

On one level, I was relieved: he hadn't beaten me up or stolen money or anything else from me, which as what Banger Bates usually did. But on another level I was really worried. What was this 'dog' business? And why me?

CHAPTER 3

I'm in Class 6M in Year 6 at Olaf Smith Junior School. Unfortunately, so is Banger Bates. Because our teacher, Miss Moore, sits us in alphabetical order, I'm on the next table to Banger, with only Ian Brown and Clare Carruthers between us. I've often thought of telling Miss Moore our family have changed their name to Zabriski so I can sit as far away from Banger as possible, but I think she'd check, so it isn't worth it.

All through the morning, while we were doing Literacy and Numbers, I kept taking a look at Banger to see if he was watching me, but he wasn't. Having given me his message, he'd dismissed me from his thoughts. Anyway, he was having enough trouble with the Literacy and Numbers work Miss

Moore had set. There's only so much one poor brain cell can do on its own, and Banger Bates's lonely brain cell struggled at the best of times.

At lunchtime as we sat in the dining hall and opened our lunch boxes, my best friend, Paul Sears, said to me, 'What was all that with Banger Bates this morning?'

'All what?' I asked.

'You kept looking at him and you had a puzzled look on your face.'

I nearly answered, 'I was trying to work out if he was human,' but decided against it in case someone told Banger what I'd said. Instead, I told Paul what had happened before the start of school.

Paul looked as baffled as I did. 'A dog?'

I nodded.

'What sort of dog?' he asked.

'I don't know,' I said. 'Don't you know?'

'Why should I know?' Paul said.

'You live just a few doors away from him. You might have seen it.'

'We live round the corner from him,' Paul pointed out. 'And I'm careful to keep away from the Bates's house.'

Paul lives on the same estate as Banger and his family, Grove Farm, about three doors away round the corner. He says that in the summer time when all the windows are open, he can hear the sound from their TV set.

Paul frowned. 'Knowing Banger Bates's family I bet it's something fierce. A rottweiler or a pit bull or something similar. Some fierce and vicious breed that kills people.'

'But why would he want me to look after it?' I asked, still bewildered.

'Because it's too dangerous for Banger,' said Paul.

The thought made me go cold with horror. Being given responsibility for a dog that was too dangerous for someone like Banger to handle ... I could feel myself go all woozy.

'What's up?' asked Paul, stuffing a sandwich into his mouth. 'You've gone a funny colour. Sort of pale.'

'I thought I was going to faint,' I explained.

'Look at the good side,' said Paul.

'What good side?'

'Today is the last day before the half-term holiday. Whatever happens, you won't have to see Banger Bates after today for a whole week.'

'Yes, but I'll have his gran's rotten dog,' I pointed out. 'A killer rottweiler or something.'

'Not if you run away,' said Paul. 'As soon as school ends, run. It's a whole week. He'll have forgotten about it soon.'

'He looked pretty serious,' I said, remembering the expression on Banger's face. 'I don't think it's the sort of thing he'd forget. For one thing, every time he looks at the dog he'll remember. And when he does he'll come round my house.'

Paul thought about it, then nodded seriously. 'You're right,' he said, and he took another giant mouthful of his sandwich and began chewing.

'How can you eat at a time like this?' I asked. 'I am facing death, either from a killer dog or from

Banger Bates.'

'I'm hungry,' said Paul. He continued eating.

I sat there in a gloomy mood, thinking of the terrible fate that lay in store for me, and my appetite vanished. I looked into my lunchbox and even though I had a sandwich made from really nice cheese and a chocolate biscuit, I couldn't eat them. The thought of the terrors that lay in store for me made my stomach heave.

'I can't eat anything,' I said unhappily.

'In that case, can I have your chocolate biscuit?' asked Paul. And before I could say 'No,' that I might feel better later, he'd whipped it out of my lunchbox and started to unwrap it. This was turning into a Bad Day.

FACTOID:
Vomit
Vomit is usually green because of a chemical called bile. Bile is used when digesting food.

Things improved slightly after lunchtime. It was Science, and Miss Moore read us a letter which the local paper had sent to all schools in our area about a Science competition.

'To help promote Science in schools, we are running a schools' Science competition,' she read. 'Entries will be limited to one Science project from each school. The deadline for submitting entries is Wednesday 16th May.'

She then pointed to the date written on the board: Friday 4th May. 'For those of you who are able to use a calendar, you will see that the deadline date is the Wednesday after we come back from the half-term holiday. So what Miss Nelson and I have decided to do is this: we will collect your entries when you come back to school on Monday 14th, and select one of them as the Science project which will represent the school. That project will be submitted to the local paper on Wednesday. The good news is it means you have a whole ten days to work on your projects and make them really exciting! Now, so I can get an idea of who's interested, put your hands up if you will be entering a Science project for the competition.'

If she was disappointed by the fact that only three hands went up out of the twenty-five children in the class, Miss Moore didn't show it. She carried on smiling. I often think that teachers lead a weird life. They have to pretend that they're really helping to educate children, and that the children appreciate this, even when it's fairly obvious to even the brain-dead that many kids haven't got any interest in school at all except as a place to play football at break.

The three of us who put up their hands were me, Paul, and a new girl in our class, Sukijeet Patel.

'Well done, you three!' enthused Miss Moore. Grabbing a sheet of paper and a pen, she called out, 'Right, tell me the titles of your projects. Dave?'

'The Human Body,' I said.

Some of the other kids sniggered at this, and I heard someone mutter, 'How to fart.' Miss Moore decided to ignore this remark, and asked, 'Sukijeet?'

'Pond Life,' replied Sukijeet.

'Excellent!' said Miss Moore. 'Paul?'

'The Planets,' said Paul.

This was so predictable of Paul. He is a complete nerd about the planets and outer space and stuff. He also loves sci-fi. I bet his project was going to consist of pictures from Star Wars. I'd beat him easily. 'The Human Body' was bound to win!

CHAPTER 4

School ends at 3.15, and the nearer the hands of the clock ticked towards that time, the more I thought about Banger Bates and his gran's terrifying dog. I had to do something to escape from this nightmare. I kept thinking: why had Banger picked on me? Why not Paul, or Barry, or Anuj, or any of the other boys in our class?

When the clock showed 3.10, I began secretly putting my pencils and books in my bag, hoping that Miss Moore wouldn't notice. My plan was to belt out of the door and run off home as fast as I could before Banger Bates could grab me. If Banger caught up with me later I'd say I'd forgotten about the dog. All right, it wasn't the best plan in the world, but it was the only one I had.

'What are you doing, Dave?' called out Miss Moore.

I looked up and saw her looking straight at me.

'Er, nothing, miss,' I said.

'Are you putting your things away?' she demanded.

'No,' I lied. 'I was getting a pen out of my bag.'

'Then where is all your stuff?'

She was right. In my eagerness to make a run for it, I'd put everything away and my table top was clear. Isn't it amazing! Most times when a teacher asks a question in class and you know the right answer and you put your hand up and wave it frantically about, they never spot you and always ask someone else. But when you don't want them to notice you because you're writing a secret note to someone, or you're picking your nose, they see everything you do, even when their back is turned!

'Take your stuff out of your bag,' she ordered.

'But, miss!' I protested.

By now the clock was showing 3.14. Everyone was looking at me. Especially Banger Bates, who had a look in his eye that showed he was almost thinking, wondering why I had packed away my things so early.

'Take everything out of your bag and put it back on your desk,' said Miss Moore firmly. 'Perhaps that

will teach you not to be so eager to get away.'

I groaned and began to unpack my bag, and as I did so, the clock's minute hand moved to 3.15 and the bell for the end of school began to ring. Immediately everyone sat up straight.

'Dave, you can stop now, and sit up straight like everyone else.'

I did as I was told, but my heart was sinking. My big plan had just failed. It would take me at least another minute or two to cram everything back into my bag, and any hope of getting away from school and Banger Bates was gone.

'Right, children, I hope you have an enjoyable half-term break,' said Miss Moore. 'And I look forward to getting your Science projects when you come back. Although only three of you have said what you will be doing, I'm sure there will be others of you who will be working on your own on your projects during next week, and I can't wait to see them. Now, off you go.'

By the time I'd finished putting everything back in

my bag, I was the last one in the classroom. I could see Banger Bates hanging about in the corridor outside, waiting for me. I wondered whether I could get out of the window and run off that way, but the windows in our classroom don't open wide enough for that. My only hope was to use Miss Moore as a cover.

I picked up my bag and went over to Miss Moore's desk, where she was putting some papers into her case.

'Can I carry your bag to the car, miss?' I offered.

She looked at me with a mixture of suspicion and surprise. 'Why?'

'Because …' I began. Then stopped while I tried to think of a reason. 'Because I thought you seemed to be suffering from a pain in your elbow.' All right, it was lame, but to try and make it sound sensible I drew on my human body project. 'Do you know there are 205 bones in the human skeleton? And the ones that are in the joints often turn painful. Especially when people get old.'

FACTOID:
Bones

The human skeleton is the frame for a body. Without it we'd be just a lump of fat and gristle. The largest bone in the human body is the thigh bone, also called the femur. The smallest bone is one in the ear called the stirrup.

As soon as I saw Miss Moore glaring at me, I knew I had said the wrong thing.

'Three things on which you are wrong, David,' she said, and her tone was not welcoming. 'One: my elbow does not hurt. Two: there are 206 bones in the human skeleton, not 205. Three: I am not old. Now, you may go.'

So, I went.

When I got outside, Banger Bates was waiting for me.

'What was all that about?' he asked.

'What was what about?' I repeated, hoping to

baffle him so he'd forget why he'd been waiting for me.

'Talking to Miss Moore.'

'I had to discuss my Science project with her,' I said.

'Well, you won't have much time for that,' he said. 'You'll be looking after my gran's dog. Come on.'

And with that, he marched off. I stayed where I was, hoping he'd keep walking and that once he'd gone round a corner I could run off. Instead, he noticed I wasn't with him, and turned and glared at me.

'Come on!' he snapped. 'Or I'll hit you!'

I groaned. I was doomed. I was going to be eaten alive by a killer dog. As I reluctantly walked towards Banger, I thought: this is not my lucky day.

CHAPTER 5

As I said, Banger Bates and his family live on the Grove Farm estate, just round the corner from Paul's house. Grove Farm sounds like something out in the country, all animals and flowers and vegetables, but actually it's a huge estate and you can easily get lost in it. The one place you can always find, though, is Banger Bates's house. It's got loads of old rusting cars in pieces in the front garden, and some of the upstairs windows are boarded up. The neighbours' houses on either side are really neat and tidy, with flowerbeds and the doors and windows nicely painted, and between them is the Bates's house, which looks like a war's been fought there.

Banger and I walked through the piles of car parts and other rubbish to the front door. The door wasn't locked. In fact it didn't have a lock on it at all, just a hole in the wood where a lock should have been. My guess was Banger or one of his bigger brothers had kicked the door in. Banger walked into the house and I hung about outside, terrified in case a huge fierce killer dog should suddenly leap up at me and start chewing. I wondered where the dog was. There was no sign of a chain or a kennel, but they could have been out the back.

'Oi, Dickens!' called Banger from inside the house. 'What are you waiting for? Come in!'

Nervously, I poked a toe in through the front door. Nothing ate it. I stepped further in. This was the first time I'd ever been inside Banger's house, and I was surprised to find that it was neat and clean. Well, at least, the parts of the house that I could see were neat and clean. The carpets in the hallway were thick and bouncy, and the walls were hung with more ornaments than I had ever seen in one place in my life, outside of a gift shop. There were pictures of Spanish villages and dancing women, dolls, and various ornaments made of brass, covering the walls with just the occasional scrap of wallpaper to be seen behind them.

There was still no sign or sound of the dog. Perhaps it was kept locked in a cellar. I pictured it, hidden below ground beneath a trapdoor, surrounded by bones. Some of them human.

Banger had disappeared into another room somewhere at the back, and I heard him say, 'Come on, you horrible mutt!'

A few seconds later, he reappeared, trailing a dog lead behind him. On the end of the lead was … well, a dog. A nothing special sort of dog. It was big, but not especially big. It didn't look very fierce. In fact, it didn't look fierce at all. It looked like a big old easy-going dog and it gazed up at me with a friendly glint in its eyes. I was puzzled. It didn't seem dangerous at all. Why did Banger want me to look after it?

Suddenly I became aware of a bad smell. No, 'bad smell' aren't the right words. This was a smell that reached new heights of badness. Rotten eggs, rotting cabbages, drains and sewers, dustbins, landfill sites, vomit, manure; this combined every putrid smell that ever was in one massive stink. It was so powerful it was almost solid. You felt you could reach out and touch it. It filled the whole house, tendrils of stench reaching out and heading for the nearest nose to fill it and render its owner unconscious.

FACTOID:
Bad Smells

The smell in farts is because of the bacteria that live in the gut. These bacteria are called Methanobacterium smithii, and they make methane gas from digesting tough foods.

'Edward!' The roar of an angry voice from somewhere upstairs made the whole house shake. 'Has that dog farted again? I warned you what would happen if you let it fart in this house!'

'No, Dad!' Banger called upstairs, and for the first time ever I saw fear in his face. 'It's a kid from school. He's always farting. That's why he's going to look after Fred while Gran's away. They'll get on well together.'

With that, Banger thrust the end of the dog lead at me and hissed, 'Get this mutt out of here! And don't bring it back. Take it round my gran's house when she gets back from Brighton next Friday.' He pushed a scrap of paper at me. 'Here's her address.'

I stood there, holding the dog's lead, stunned. A farting dog! And not just any old farting dog, but a champion farter!

'Well?' demanded Banger. 'What are you waiting for?'

'I can't take this dog home,' I protested. 'My mum and dad will kill me.' Not to mention Krystal.

'If you don't, I'll kill you,' snarled Banger.

'But .... but .... How does your gran cope with the farting?' I asked, hoping for some useful advice.

'She doesn't notice,' said Banger. 'She's got no sense of smell. Now go on, go away. And take that thing with you!'

The next second, I found myself back outside the Bates's house among the old car parts and piles of rubbish, looking at a closed front door and holding a dog on the end of a lead.

I looked down at the dog, and he looked up at me with his big old friendly face.

'Well, Fred,' I said. 'I guess it's you and me.'

At these words, Fred the dog wagged his tail. Unfortunately, he let out a silent fart at the same time, so his wagging tail wafted the smell even further afield. My Unlucky Day had just got a whole lot worse.

FACTOID:
Farts

The methane and hydrogen gas in farts can catch fire very easily. On average a person will produce half a litre of fart gas every day.

CHAPTER 6

As I trudged home with Fred plodding along on the lead by my side, I felt as if an angel of doom was hovering above me. In the space of one day, my whole life had collapsed completely. Life had been great the day before because I was going to collect twenty pounds just for doing nothing. I only had to avoid upsetting my family by doing anything they might consider disgusting.

Now, less than twenty-four hours later, I was about to arrive home with an animal whose gastric expulsion system could provide enough methane to power a small city. And what was worse, he farted silently, which meant people might think the smell was coming from me! My family certainly would. And even if I persuaded them it wasn't me who was farting, I would get the blame for bringing this dog into the house! The twenty pounds was vanishing even as I thought about it.

It did occur to me that I could abandon Fred; take him off the lead and remove his collar so no one would know who he was, and just let him go. But he had such a kind face with such big appealing eyes that I couldn't do that to him. Plus there was the fact that when Banger found out Fred was missing, he'd bash me up.

There was always the hope that Fred wouldn't fart at all while he was at my house, but he'd already let off a couple of juicy ones as we walked along the road, causing a man with a moustache to glare at me and mutter, 'How dare you, foul child!' and a lollipop lady to fall into a hedge.

I was trapped.

When I got home I decided to play things carefully. I tied Fred's lead to an ornamental garden gnome that Dad had decided would improve our tiny front garden. Then I went into the kitchen and found

Mum on the phone.

'He's never usually this late,' she was saying, and then she turned and saw me. 'It's all right, he's here. I'm sorry to have troubled you. 'Bye.'

She hung up and glared at me, angry. I was being glared at a lot today.

'Where have you been?' she demanded. 'I've been worried out of my mind.'

'I had to go and get a dog,' I said.

Mum looked at me as if I was talking in a strange language she didn't understand.

'A dog?' she repeated.

'Yes,' I nodded. 'A dog. It belongs to a very old lady and she needs someone to look after it for her while she's away for a week.'

'What sort of dog?' asked Mum suspiciously.

'It's an old dog called Fred. Very gentle.'

Mum kept looking at me, a suspicious expression on her face. 'Why you?'

'Because there's no one else to help her,' I said.

Mum was obviously trying to work out what was

really going on. After a while, she repeated, just to make things absolutely clear, 'A dog?'

'Yes,' I nodded. 'An old dog called Fred.'

'And where is this dog?'

'I've left him outside for the moment,' I said.

Mum headed for the door, with me following. She opened it and saw Fred sitting patiently tied to the garden gnome. When he saw us, he stood up and began wagging his tail, with his most appealing big-eyed friendly look.

'There,' I said. 'That's Fred.'

'Why, he's .... he's lovely,' she said, surprised. Still with that same tone of surprise, she turned to me and demanded, 'Why didn't you ever tell us you wanted a dog?'

'I don't,' I said. 'I'm just looking after it for this old lady for a week.'

Just then there was the sound of a car pulling up, and Dad's car turned into the driveway. He got out and saw me and Mum standing next to Fred.

'What's going on?' he asked. 'What's that dog doing there?'

Mum gave me a proud smile. 'Our son here has done a wonderful thing,' she said. 'He has offered to look after this poor old dog for a poor little old lady who's had to go into hospital for a week, or something.'

This surprised me. I'd never mentioned that Banger Bates's gran was little or poor, just that she was very old. I'd certainly never said anything about her having to go into hospital, but whatever had put that idea into Mum's head I decided to go along with it. So far everything seemed to be going fine.

Dad looked at me, equally impressed. 'Dave, that is a wonderful thing you've done,' he said. 'Many children of your age would spend their half term messing about and getting into trouble. But for you to do something as unselfish as this for some poor old lady …'

Words failed him and he gave Mum a proud smile. I even thought I saw a tear in his eye. This was going so well!

And then Fred farted.

FACTOID:
Farts

Really smelly farts are usually quieter than ordinary farts, because of bacteria. Bacteria in the digestive system produces heat as well as gas. Warm farts are generally quieter than cold farts, and it is the bacteria in them that makes them smell a lot worse.

CHAPTER 7

The effect of Fred's fart was astonishing to see. As the smell hit Mum, she put one hand over her mouth and nose, clutched at her throat with the other and stumbled backwards, a look of shock in her eyes. For Dad it was even worse. His eyes crossed and all colour drained out of his face, and then he collapsed on the ground.

Fred, seeing this, did what most dogs would do in the circumstances: he rushed over to the fallen Dad to see if he was all right. Unfortunately he pulled the ornamental garden gnome off its concrete base and brought it with him and, as he ran, the gnome bounced over the stone pathway and pieces fell off; namely a fishing rod and the gnome's big nose.

Mum was the first to recover. She turned on me,

and now all traces of pride had gone from her face. 'What have you been eating?' she demanded.

'It wasn't me!' I said defensively. 'It was the dog.'

Mum gave me her 'How dare you' look, and said angrily, 'It's bad enough that you do that sort of anti-social thing, but to blame a poor defenceless animal …'

At that moment Dad returned to consciousness and began to sit up. Unfortunately for him, Fred had heard the angry tone in my mum's voice and turned towards her, putting his tail end right by Dad's face. As Dad was now sitting on the ground, this meant his nose was at dog's bum-level from the ground, so that when Fred let off another one …

'Aaarghhh!' shouted Dad, and he leapt to his feet and ran for his car to take shelter from the smell. This yell of alarm only made poor Fred worry even more about Dad and he hurried after him, causing more pieces of the garden gnome to fall off.

'It is the dog!' groaned Dad hoarsely, his words muffled because he had his hands over his mouth and nose.

'What?' demanded Mum.

'The dog,' said Dad again, pointing at Fred, who looked up at him and wagged his tail, obviously relieved to see this strange man hadn't suffered any serious injury. 'It made that smell.' Then his eyes took in the fragments of garden gnome scattered over the ground and he gaped in horror. 'And it's smashed my best garden gnome!'

Mum fixed me with a grim look. 'Tie that dog up and then come inside,' she said firmly. 'We need to talk.'

This time I tied Fred to the gatepost. Then I went inside and joined Mum and Dad in the kitchen where they sat waiting for me. The grim looks on their faces told me their admiration for my unselfish deed had vanished.

'Did you do this on purpose?' demanded my mum.

'Do what?'

'Bring home this animal that makes these dreadful smells.'

'No,' I said. 'I didn't know it did that sort of thing when I said I'd look after it.'

Which was true. When Banger had first grabbed me about looking after the dog, that was one thing he definitely hadn't mentioned.

'It can't stay here,' said Dad. 'We can't have that smell hanging around the house. The council will take action against us under the Noxious Smells Act. It's also unhygienic. You've got to take the dog back to this old woman, whoever she is, and tell her you can't look after it.'

'But she isn't at home,' I said. 'Not for a week.'

'No, she's in hospital,' nodded Mum.

I could have said, 'No she isn't, she's in Brighton', but I decided to keep my mouth shut. That way I wasn't lying. (Although, deep down, I knew I was.)

'Well surely she must have relatives who can look after it,' insisted Dad.

I decided this was a useful time to tell the truth. Well, some of the truth.

'Yes, she does,' I said. 'They live on Grove Farm just

a few doors away from Paul, and they're horrible. Their house is a mess and they're always in trouble with the council. They bully people. Even the police are too scared to call at their house.'

FACTOID:
Rubbish

Some litter can take a long time to break down. A plastic bag can take ten years, and a drink can might take up to a hundred years, Some litter can also be dangerous. Plastic fishing lines can strangle animals and birds. Small animals can get trapped inside plastic bags and suffocate.

Mum nodded. 'And this old lady doesn't want her dog being looked after by them, I bet. Being beaten and starved.'

I didn't say Yes and I didn't say No. I just gave her one of those sad and sympathetic looks that meant, 'You are so right.'

'But there has to be someone else!' said Dad desperately. 'Isn't there some sort of animal charity that can look after it?'

'There's the dogs' home,' I said, adding unhappily, 'but I hear they put the dogs to sleep if they're not claimed after four days.'

This was a rumour that Paul had once told me. I'd found out it wasn't actually true, but these were tough times, and I had to use every weapon if I was going to come out of this without being beaten up by Banger Bates. And also with twenty pounds from Dad.

'It can't go into a dogs' home,' said Mum firmly.

'But we can't have it in the house,' insisted Dad. 'We'll never get the smell out of the curtains!'

'I can make Fred a kennel in the back garden,' I suggested. 'He can stay there.'

'Not much fun for him, being chained up all the time,' said Mum.

'Better than being put to sleep,' Dad pointed out. 'But who's going to take it for walks? Clean up after it? Feed it?'

'Me,' I said.

There was a pause, and then Mum looked at Dad and said, 'It's either that or the dog goes to this old lady's relatives who'll be cruel to it.'

I could see from Dad's unhappy face that, as far as he was concerned, this was a better option than having Fred polluting the area in and around our house. However, Mum had spoken.

'All right,' he said. 'But I want you to do your best

to stop the creature making those dreadful smells. Is that clear?'

I nodded.

'Don't worry,' I said. 'I'm already on it.'

CHAPTER 8

And I was on the problem. I know from my Science researches that it's the gases in our insides which make us fart and belch, and those gases are affected by what we eat. There are so many fascinating facts about farts. On average a person produces half a litre of fart gas every day! That much gas will make about twelve farts. The thing that makes farts smell is the bacteria living in our guts. This bacteria is necessary to break down food but it also makes methane gas, and when methane gas is mixed with sulphide and other things, that's what gives the smell! Farts also contain hydrogen, and methane and hydrogen are both very flammable. Which means, if you fart too near a fire there is a danger of your bum catching alight.

These are just a few of the amazing facts about farts and farting, and I had already started writing about them as part of my human body Science project for Miss Moore. Now I saw an even better way to use this knowledge: to try and stop Fred farting! If I could do that then maybe I could hand him back to Banger Bates ahead of time, and so make sure of getting my hands on that twenty pounds Dad had promised me.

Once we'd got over the upset of Dad and Mum finding out about Fred, and the destruction of Dad's favourite garden gnome, I decided it would be best if I stayed out of their way. I spent the evening putting together a makeshift kennel for Fred outside, while Fred sat down and watched. Actually, it wasn't really a kennel, more of a tent which I'd rigged up from an old tarpaulin, but Fred seemed pleased with it. I was putting a blanket inside it for him to lie on when Krystal appeared round the side of the house with her friend, Shelly.

Shelly is in the same class as Krystal at school, but

she is nicer than my sister. Actually, anyone would have to try really hard to be worse than my sister, so that's not saying much. While Krystal terrifies most living things, human or animal, Shelly is generally kind to them. (Actually, it's not just humans and animals that Krystal terrifies. I have seen flowers drop down and hide in long grass when Krystal comes near them.) What's strange is that Krystal thinks Shelly is the best person in the whole world.

She thinks that Shelly is some kind of multi-talented genius, just because she once appeared on one of those TV talent shows when she was ten.

My own view is that Shelly, although harmless (unlike my sister), is a bit of an airhead. She's always smiling and saying how lovely things are, even when they're not. She's the kind of person who'd arrive at the scene of an earthquake, see the flattened buildings and start talking about a lovely opportunity for re-decoration.

Krystal was the first one round the corner, and when she saw Fred she stopped in her tracks and demanded, 'What's that animal doing here?' in a tone that told me my life was in serious danger.

Shelly, however, gave a little squeal of joy and said, 'Oh, what a lovely dog!' She hurried over to Fred to pat him on the head and make a fuss of him. This completely changed Krystal's attitude and she went to join Shelly at Fred's side.

'Actually,' I said nervously, 'I wouldn't get too close.'

'Oh, I'm not frightened of dogs!' said Shelly cheerily. 'I love animals, and they love me!'

And she rubbed Fred's ears. Fred thought all this fuss being made of him was wonderful, so he stood up and began to wag his tail happily. Krystal, who is usually suspicious of anything with four legs, decided that if this friendly behaviour was good for Shelly, it was good for her, and she began to scratch Fred on the back. Whether it was Krystal's scratching that did it, or whether it was just Fred's intestinal clock due for another eruption, but both girls suddenly staggered back. Initially their mouths were open in shock, but then they soon shut them tight. Shelly began staggering around, flailing her hands wildly to try and drive away the smell. Krystal just came straight for me, fists bunched and a look on her face that would have terrified Genghis Khan.

I didn't wait to explain the situation, but belted indoors as fast as I could and spent the next quarter of an hour standing as close to Mum as possible without actually being glued to her.

This caused Mum some annoyance as she was on the phone to her sister, and every now and then she'd hiss at me, 'What do you want?' and 'Go away, I'm on the phone!'

All the time I kept my eyes on the window and what was happening outside. Shelly was now being sick on the lawn and Krystal was giving Fred one of her terrifying glares and pointing at him. Amazingly, Fred didn't seem upset by this. He just wagged his tail, which only made Krystal worse.

FACTOID:
Vomit
Horses, rabbits, rats and mice are the only mammals that don't vomit.

Finally the two girls came into the house. Shelly, who was looking for once as if everything in life wasn't totally wonderful, headed straight upstairs to the bathroom, and Krystal made for the kitchen, looking for me with murderous intent. I huddled closer to Mum, which made her even angrier so that she shouted at both me and Krystal to leave her in peace to talk on the phone.

Krystal gave me a hard stare and hissed menacingly, 'I'll see you later!' before going upstairs to see if Shelly was all right.

I nipped outside and put the finishing touches to Fred's tent. He came over and nuzzled me with his big head, giving me his lopsided smile.

'Don't worry, Fred, I'm not angry with you,' I sighed. 'It wasn't your fault. And I'm sorry you've got to stay outside, but it's only until we get your digestive system sorted out.'

FACTOID:
Digestion
The human stomach makes enough acid to dissolve a bone in just a few hours. The human body makes about 8 litres a day of this acid digestive juice.

Fred seemed to understand, because he trotted inside the tent and lay down on the blanket I'd put inside it. I'd put him on a long chain so he could walk around. I didn't really like tying him up, but I didn't want him running off and disappearing. I put down a bowl of water and a bowl of dog food, and then sat on the back step and watched him eat and drink. Not that watching a dog eat is my idea of entertainment, but the alternative was to go inside

the house and risk bumping into the mad Krystal.

After a while I heard raised voices inside the house and realised it was Krystal complaining about me and the dog to Mum and Dad, and Mum and Dad trying to calm her down while they explained the situation with Fred. I decided to stay out of it. If I'd tried to say all that to Krystal she'd have torn my arms off and made me eat them.

Finally there was silence, then Krystal appeared at the back door and scowled at me. 'Mum and Dad say I'm not to have a go at you. They say you're doing some good deed for some old lady who's in hospital.'

She thrust her face close to mine. I gulped and moved back in case she bit me. 'But you don't fool me!' she snarled. 'I know you did this on purpose to get your disgusting revenge on me! Well if you or that revolting dog come anywhere near me, I shall kill both of you! Is that clear?'

Because I was too terrified to say anything, I nodded.

Then Shelly appeared behind Krystal, and said, 'I'm better now,' in that shiny happy voice of hers – although I thought she sounded weaker than normal – and both of them went off. I noticed that this time they didn't say goodbye to Fred.

CHAPTER 9

The next day, Saturday, I put my Stop Fred Farting plan into operation. Because Dad, Mum and especially Krystal spent breakfast time giving me nasty looks, I decided to spend as little time in the house with them as possible. I clipped on Fred's lead and we set off for the park. One of Fred's problems was that he couldn't be going for enough walks. If you don't get enough exercise, the food in your gut doesn't move along fast enough; it just sits there and gets rancid and smelly. This was one of the reasons why Fred's farts were so powerful.

On the way, I called in at Paul's, being careful to take a back way round the estate so as not to pass Banger's house. Paul looked at me in surprise when he opened the door. 'You're up early,' he said.

'Yes,' I said. 'I'm taking the dog to the park for a walk.'

Paul looked at Fred. 'Is that Banger Bates's dog?'

'Yes,' I said. 'He's called Fred.'

'He doesn't look very dangerous to me,' he said, sounding disappointed. He opened the door wider.

'Are you coming in?' he asked.

At that moment Fred farted, a silent but extremely deadly fart, which made Paul rock back on his heels. 'Wow!' he said.

'Do you want me to come in?' I asked.

'No,' said Paul firmly. 'I'll get my coat.'

As we walked along, I noticed that Paul had brought his school bag.

'What's in the bag?' I asked.

'My Science project,' said Paul. 'I've got loads of stuff I need to sort out. I was going to start on it this morning, so I might as well bring it with me. I couldn't stay in the house with that dog.'

Fred seemed unaffected by Paul's remarks. He trotted alongside us on his lead, quite happily.

'What did your mum and dad say when they saw him?' asked Paul.

'They were upset at first, but I think they're getting used to it,' I said. Then I thought about it and added, 'Except for Dad. Fred broke his favourite garden gnome.'

Paul shook his head. 'A garden gnome! There are some strange people about.'

The park wasn't too busy, but that's because it was a Saturday morning. Later in the day, the football-

playing crowd would turn up and take it over. And then, later still, the drunks would arrive and sit drinking cans of strong ale and bottles of vodka. Saturday morning was the safest time to be in the park. All you had to put up with were the joggers, running around holding their bottles of energy drink and listening to music on their headphones.

FACTOID:
Sweat
Sweat itself doesn't smell. The bad smell that goes with sweat is caused by bacteria growing on the skin, these bacteria increasing when sweat is added. Sweat is mostly water with some minerals.

Paul and I sat down on one of the benches and I let Fred off his lead so he could go and have a run, but he didn't seem interested. He preferred hanging about near us and sniffing at the grass.

'What are you going to do with the dog?' asked Paul.

'I'm going to take care of him for the week, and I'm going to try and stop him farting.'

As if he'd heard me, Fred let off one of his juicy ones. Luckily for us, he was a fair distance away from the bench, but a hint of the smell drifted towards us on the breeze. I noticed a jogger who was running past Fred at the time stumble and nearly fall, but he recovered his balance and staggered on.

'How are you going to do that?' asked Paul.

'Diet and exercise,' I said.

'Why?' asked Paul. 'This is Banger Bates's dog. Why are you doing something nice for Banger Bates? He's a bully and a thug and he's nasty to everybody.'

'Fred isn't Banger Bates's dog, he's his gran's,' I pointed out. 'For all I know she might be a really nice person. If Fred's anything to go by, she is. He's not vicious or snarling or anything. In fact, he's very good-natured, which makes me think the person he's with most of the time is also good-natured. Dangerous rotten dogs have dangerous rotten owners. Besides, I like Fred and I want to help him.'

Paul shook his head. 'I think you're mad,' he said. 'All the time you spend on that dog means you won't be spending it doing your Science project, and we've got to hand them in next Monday.'

'True,' I agreed, 'but I've got a lot of my project already worked out. I only have to write it up and do some diagrams. I can still get it done in time.'

I'm sure I sounded confident, but the truth was, I was worried. Looking after Fred meant I would have to spend a lot of time outside so his farts could be blown away in the air, and the more time I spent outside, the less time I'd have to work on my project.

'Anyway, we can take turns,' I suggested.

Paul gave me a puzzled look. 'Take turns at what?' he asked.

'Looking after Fred.'

Paul looked even more puzzled. 'Why would I want to take turns looking after a farting dog?'

'Because you're my best friend,' I said. 'That's what

best friends do.'

'Not with a dog that farts like that.'

He opened his bag and took out a book. 'Look,' he said proudly. 'My mum bought me this yesterday when we went shopping.'

I looked. The book was called *The Solar System* and had a glossy picture of Saturn with its rings on the front cover.

'It's fantastic!' Paul told me. 'There's everything in here I need to do a brilliant project!' He opened it up and showed me some of the pictures and information inside. Photos and coloured drawings of planets. A plan of the Solar System. Pictures of meteors flying through the night sky.

'It's got a whole section on black holes!' Paul said. 'And different galaxies!'

'You're just going to copy it?' I demanded.

'Maybe bits of it,' he admitted. 'Anyway, it's no worse than taking stuff off the Internet, which is what you do.'

'No, I don't,' I protested. 'I get loads of different

facts and compare them. I don't just copy things – I carry out experiments, and make tests, and look at specimens under the microscope.'

'Yes, well, you can't do that with planets and universes,' said Paul defensively. 'You can't put them under a microscope.'

'Then it's not real Science,' I protested. 'It's copying Science! Your project isn't a proper Science project at all! It's a cheat!'

Paul stood up and looked at me, angry and hurt. 'I'm not a cheat! And if that's what you think, then you're not a real friend of mine.'

He pushed the book back in his bag. 'In fact, as far as I'm concerned, you're not my friend any more.'

I sat on the bench and fumed. How dare he say that to me? Me, who had been his best friend since we'd started school together when we were both five. Me, who had helped him with his Arithmetic homework when we were in Mrs Thomson's class. All right, he'd got it all wrong because my answers had been wrong, but that wasn't the point. I'd helped him then because I was his friend.

'If that's how you feel, then that's the way it is,' I said, equally angry. 'If you were my friend you'd help me look after Fred, instead of taking advantage of this rotten situation just so you can win the Science competition with a copied project. But that's what you're doing because you're not really a friend.'

Paul stood glaring at me, his face all white and his mouth shut tight, and for a moment I thought he might do something silly, like hit me. But then he grabbed his bag to his chest and said, 'Goodbye, ex-friend.' Then he walked off, narrowly avoiding being run down by a jogger as he went.

I sat on the bench and watched him go, wondering if he was going to turn around and look at me. If he did, I wondered what I'd do. Would I just turn away and ignore him? Or would I stand up and go after him and tell him not to be silly? As it was, he didn't turn back; he just walked out of the park.

As I watched him disappear, I felt something damp against my knee. I looked down. It was Fred, pushing his big head against me. I guessed he'd had enough of being out in the big wide world and wanted to go home and eat something.

I sighed. 'We can't go home just yet, Fred,' I told him. 'It won't be safe until Krystal leaves the house, and she usually goes out on Saturday afternoons.' I put his lead back on him and stood up. 'Tell you what, we'll take a walk around the park. It'll do us both good.'

With that, we set off. As we did, Fred farted again.

CHAPTER 10

Next day was Sunday. Fred sat in his tent during the morning and occasionally farted, while I finally got the chance to do some research for my human body project, looking at interesting stuff, like dandruff, under my microscope. In fact some of the stuff I saw, like bacteria, was so fascinating that I even thought of taking my microscope round to Paul's house and showing him. Then I thought about the bad things we'd said to one another the day before, and decided against it.

I took Fred for a walk in the afternoon, just to keep him exercised and help his bowels keep moving. When he did a poo on the pavement, I scooped it up it in a plastic bag so I could put it into a dog-poo bin. Everyone has to do this by law because there are parasites in dog poo that are really dangerous. Most dogs have worms in their stomachs, and these worms lay eggs that come out in the dog poo. If you touch dog poo with your hands and then lick your fingers, these eggs can get inside you and can cause blindness. OK, most people don't lick their fingers if they touch dog poo, even accidentally, but babies and little kids do because they lick everything, and that's why you have to clean up after your dog.

FACTOID:
Poo

About a third of a poo is dead bacteria. Another third is the stuff the stomach couldn't digest. This is called cellulose and helps the poo move along the gut because it gives the muscles of your gut something to grip on to.

The problem was that, unlike in the park, the nearest dog-poo bin was quite a way away, and if struck me that if anyone saw me walking along carrying a plastic bag with a lump of dog poo inside it, they might complain to Mum and Dad about me, and my chance of getting hold of the twenty pounds that Dad and promised me would vanish. So I took a paper bag from my pocket that had a couple of sweets left in it, ate the sweets, and then put the plastic poo bag inside the paper bag. The paper bag actually had the name of the sweetshop printed on it, so I knew it would make a perfect disguise.

Unfortunately, I bumped into Banger Bates almost immediately. He was out with three of his mates who went to the High School. All of them were as bad as Banger, only older. Jaz was twelve, and Mick and Pod were thirteen. You'd have thought that as the other three were older than Banger, one of them would be the one who gave orders, but Banger was actually the leader of the gang. My guess was that because Banger was bigger than the others, he was more dangerous, and they were also frightened of Banger's dad.

'Dickens!' yelled Banger. 'Still looking after the farting dog?' And he laughed out loud. It was a sound like a drain being cleared. The other three joined in the laughter.

Then Banger saw the bag in my hand and his eyes lit up. 'Yo! Sweets!' he said. 'Give 'em to me!'

'No—' I began, starting to explain they weren't sweets, but Banger didn't give me a chance. He scowled nastily and growled, 'Don't you say no to me, you little squirt!'

And with that he grabbed the bag from my hand.

I decided not to hang around any longer, because you didn't need to be a fortune-teller to guess what was going to happen next. As I hurried off with Fred, I heard Banger crow, 'See the scaredy cat run!'

Then he held out the paper bag to Pod and said, 'Go on, have some!' I looked over my shoulder and saw Pod put his hand in the paper bag, before giving a disgusted yell of 'Urgh!!'

I didn't stay around to see and hear any more but ran off as fast as I could, dragging Fred along with me. I don't think the poor old dog's legs had ever moved so fast. Banger shouted angrily after me, 'Dickens! You're dead!'

FACTOID:
Poo
Water in poo is absorbed by the body as it passes through the intestines. This means that the longer a poo stays inside the body, the drier it will be, and the harder to push out. Diarrhoea is very watery poo.

Next morning came the Shock. Fred was outside, chained in his tent, and Krystal and I were having breakfast while Dad ran around like a maniac, looking for his appointments book. Dad's a plumber and he's always losing the book that tells him where's he's supposed to be.

'I'm late!' he complained. 'I can't find my book.'

'Have you looked in the van?' asked Mum.

'Yes,' said Dad. 'That was the first place I looked.' Then he stood there, thinking. 'No, I didn't,' he admitted. 'It could well be there. I think I put it on the passenger seat.'

'Good,' said Mum. 'Oh, by the way, don't forget that my mum's coming this evening to stay for a bit.'

I was eating a bowl of cereal and Krystal was eating a slice of toast. Both of us stopped dead when we heard these words, Krystal's hand holding the toast frozen in mid air, and my spoonful of cereal hovering in front of my open mouth. We put down our untasted food. This news was enough to turn breakfast into ashes in our mouths.

To explain: Mum's mum – our gran – is one of the most terrifying people on the planet. Krystal is bad, but Gran is far, far worse. And she's tougher. She's about two hundred years old and is always complaining about her bad health and how ill she is, but I'd bet on her against any world-wrestling champion any time. Some idiot kid once tried to mug her; she knocked him unconscious with her shopping bag and then sat on him until the police came.

Whenever Gran sees me and Krystal, she moans about us. She says that I'm disgusting, and that Krystal is lazy and wears too much make-up. And that's just for starters. Any time she spends at our house, she follows Dad and Mum around telling them what awful children we are and how if she were in charge of us she'd soon straighten us out. She also complains about Dad as well. I once heard her tell Mum that she'd married beneath her. I was puzzled by this at first, because Dad's taller than Mum. Then Krystal explained this meant that Gran

thought Dad wasn't good enough for Mum, and she'd have preferred it if Mum had married someone rich.

Anyway, Krystal and I sat at the table and let this dreadful news sink in. Dad was obviously just as unhappy about the news. He frowned, then said, 'Why?' in a nervous tone of voice.

'Because it's half term,' said Mum. 'And, with you and me at work, we thought it would be a good idea to have her stay here to keep an eye on Krystal and Dave.'

'No, we didn't!' protested Dad.

'Yes, we did,' said Mum.

'We didn't!' argued Dad.

'We did!' insisted Mum.

'Dave and I can look after ourselves,' put in Krystal.

I said nothing because I know better than to interfere in an argument with Mum and Dad – although they call it 'a difference of opinion' – but for once Krystal and I were on the same side. Even a short visit from Gran was to be avoided at all costs, and having her stay with us would add to the nightmare that my life was becoming.

'Your dad and I will feel better if there's a responsible adult here during the day when we're not around to look after you,' said Mum.

'OK,' nodded Krystal, 'but can't she only be here

during the day? Does she have to be here at night as well?' Mum gave her an angry look, so she added hastily, 'I'm only thinking of Gran. After all, we've only got one bathroom, and she always says she needs to use the loo all the time. It wouldn't be fair to her if she couldn't get in because one of us was already in it.'

This was a pretty lame cover-up on Krystal's part, and it didn't cut any ice with Mum. 'My mother should be treated with respect by you children,' she said firmly. 'She is your gran, after all.'

She then turned to Dad and said, 'But Krystal's right about us only having one bathroom. You're a plumber. We need a separate toilet in this house.'

Dad groaned and shot Krystal a sour look. 'I'll look into it,' he said. Then he picked up his sandwich box and headed for the door. 'I'll see you all later.'

After he'd gone, Krystal and I returned to our breakfast. The shock had worn off, so we could start eating again without choking. I could see from Krystal's thoughtful expression that she was already trying to think up ways of keeping out of the house and out of Gran's way. I had the perfect excuse, luckily: a farting dog to look after. Mum would expect me to keep it away from Gran, and that was what I intended to do.

CHAPTER 11

Once again I took Fred to the park. It struck me that I'd spent more time in the park over the last couple of days than I had in months. But the choice was either take Fred to the park, or wander round the streets with him, or stay at home. Out of these three, the park was the safest option. This time I took my human body project with me, so that at least I could read it through and see what other information I needed.

As I was walking across the grass, I heard someone shout 'No, Anwar!' and looked round just in time to be bashed in the face by a football.

Ow!

I fell over. Fred got excited and started running around. At least, he tried to run around but I still had his lead in my hand, which meant he got tangled up in it and fell on me. Luckily for me, I recovered quickly enough to turn my head away and covered my nose and mouth with my free hand, because I realised that an excited Fred would be bound to do what he usually did.

'Cor! What a pong!'

I looked up. A small boy was standing looking down, at me holding his nose.

'It's not me, it's the dog!' I said crossly, scrambling to my feet.

By now a girl had hurried to join us, and I recognised her as the new girl in our class: Sukijeet Patel.

'I'm terribly sorry!' she said, looking really upset. 'I told Anwar to watch where he was kicking the ball. Are you hurt?'

What a stupid question! I'd just been hit in the face by a fast-moving football and knocked to the ground. Of course I was hurt!

'Yes,' I said, and showed her where the ball had hit me on the side of my face. 'Is there a bruise?'

She peered at my face. 'I don't think so.'

'It might come out later,' I said. 'That's what sometimes happens with bruises. It depends on the blood cells beneath the skin. Sometimes they go into shock at first and don't release the burst blood until later.'

'I didn't know that,' she said.

'It's part of my human body Science project,' I said, picking up my bag from where it had fallen. 'I came here to work on it.'

She looked gloomy. 'I came here to do my Science project,' she said. 'Pond Life. Only the pond is shut.'

That puzzled me. 'How can you shut a pond?'

'The council have put a fence round it and a notice saying no one's allowed to go near,' she said. 'It's because of Health and Safety.'

FACTOID:
Contaminated Water

Some polluted water has parasites in it. These are tiny little animals that can get inside the human body and lay their eggs in the stomach. These eggs hatch out and the creatures then live inside the human, feeding off it, and often making them seriously ill.

'Well, find another pond,' I said.

She gave a deep sigh. 'I can't. We live in a block of flats on the Grove Farm estate and there's no pond there. I don't know where any other ponds are, and I can't go around looking because I've got to take care of my little brother.'

She indicated the boy, who was now kicking his football a bit away from us against a tree. 'He's terrible. He's always getting into trouble. Like hitting you with his football. He doesn't mean it, but he tears around and doesn't look where he's going or what he's doing. Yesterday he nearly got run over when he ran out in the road.'

'You should keep him on a lead,' I suggested, gesturing at Fred. 'Like I do with this dog.'

'I can't put my brother on a lead!' she protested. 'People will report me for cruelty.' She looked really miserable. 'It's because my mum and dad both work and there's no one else to look after him during the day, so I have to. It's such a pain! I can't get on with my Science project.'

'Ha!' I snorted. 'You think you've got problems.' Again, I indicated Fred. 'I've got stuck with looking after this dog for the week, which means I can't get on with my Science project either!'

'Yes, but a dog isn't as bad as a little brother,' insisted Sukijeet.

'This dog is,' I said. 'He makes bad smells all the time, so I have to keep him out of the house.'

Just then we heard an angry shout: 'Get out of there!'

We both turned and saw the park ranger heading towards a bush; poking out of it was a pair of feet.

'Oh no!' groaned Sukijeet, and shouted, 'Anwar! Come here!'

The small figure of Anwar emerged from the depths of the bush, clutching his football, and ran over to us with the ranger in hot pursuit. Anwar hid behind Sukijeet as the ranger reached us. He was a young guy with muscles bulging under his shirt, the sort who works out and keeps fit. I thought he was overdoing it, throwing his weight around and menacing a small kid, but then I remembered the ball smacking me in the face and thought maybe Anwar deserved a scare.

'What do you think you were doing to that bush?' the ranger demanded.

'I was just getting my football back,' said Anwar.

'That's vandalism!' said the ranger angrily. 'You were damaging council property!'

'I'm very sorry,' said Sukijeet. 'He didn't mean any harm. He's only six years old.'

'Youth is no excuse for vandalism!' snapped the ranger. He bent down and glared at Anwar, who moved even further behind Sukijeet. 'If he goes in the bushes again, I'll have you banned from this park. Is that clear?'

'Yes, sir,' said Sukijeet unhappily. 'I'll see he doesn't.'

'Make sure you do,' scowled the ranger. He gave Anwar one last glare, then walked away.

'Oh Anwar!' groaned Sukijeet.

'It wasn't my fault,' protested her brother. 'The ball bounced the wrong way.'

Sukijeet shook her head. 'My life is a disaster! I'll never get my project done this week, with no pond to look at.'

'We've got a pond,' I said. Even as I spoke the

words, I regretted them. What on earth made me say that?

Sukijeet looked at me, sudden hope in her eyes. 'You've got a pond?' she echoed.

'In our garden. It's only a small one,' I added hastily.

'That doesn't matter,' she said. 'It's about the life that's in it, not how big it is.' And she smiled. 'Can I come and see it?'

FACTOID:
WATER

In London and many other major cities, water is recycled. It has been worked out that if you drink a glass of tap water in London then nine other people have drunk that same water before you did.

What could I say? No? How cruel would that be? I started trying to think up some excuses about why she couldn't come round – my gran was staying with us and she was mad and dangerous, or the council

might ban Sukijeet from our pond as well because of Health and Safety – but I couldn't think of anything that sounded convincing. So instead I found myself saying, 'OK,' and telling her my address.

'That's brilliant!' she said. 'When shall I —?'

But at that moment, I saw Banger and his gang walking by the flowerbeds, and realised that if they saw me I'd be in for a severe kicking after what had happened with the bag of dog poo, so I quickly said, 'I've got to go. Sorry!'

With that I pulled Fred's lead and hurried towards

the entrance. Behind me, Sukijeet called out, 'I'll come round this afternoon.'

'Right,' I replied, but not too loudly, because I didn't want Banger and his mates to recognise my voice. Luckily for me, Fred and I made it to the park gates before they spotted us.

What with flying footballs and Banger and his gang, it occurred to me the park was becoming a dangerous place.

CHAPTER 12

All the way home, I kept thinking what an idiot I was to tell Sukijeet Patel about our pond. Paul was getting loads of time to work on his Planets project; now I was helping her with Pond Life, while my own Science project was in big trouble because of the time I had to spend looking after Fred! Everything was going wrong for me this week.

Things didn't go any better when I got home. As I walked in the back way with Fred, Krystal leapt out from behind the door and grabbed me by my hair. She'd obviously been lying in wait for me.

'Gran's here!' she hissed. 'I'm going to persuade her and Mum that she doesn't need to stay. If you do anything to spoil my plan, I'll kill you and feed the bits to that dog. Is that clear?'

I was about to nod and say, 'Yes', which is hard when someone's holding you by the hair, but is generally the safest thing to do with Krystal, when Fred farted.

Krystal immediately recoiled and let go of my hair. 'Yuk!' she said, holding her nose. 'You'd better keep that dog out of her way.'

I sighed, took Fred to his tent and chained him up. 'I'm sorry for treating you like this,' I said to him. 'But until we get your farting sorted out, you can't come in the house. Dad's promised me twenty pounds if I don't do anything disgusting for a week, and if you fart in the house he might use that as an excuse not to pay me. Even though it wouldn't be me doing it! And I can't leave you outside without chaining you up, in case you run off.'

Fred gave me a friendly look, wagged his tail, and lay down. He didn't seem too upset about being on the chain.

Mum was in the kitchen making sandwiches.

'Where's Gran?' I asked.

'She's just putting her things in your room,' she answered. 'You're going to be in the attic.'

The attic! I shuddered at the thought. The attic is right at the top of our house and it's dark and gloomy and there are always strange sounds coming from it: mysterious bangs and bumps. If I wasn't a scientist, I'd think the attic was haunted. But because I'm a scientist, I don't believe in ghosts. (Most of the time.) It's so unfair that when anyone comes to stay it's me who has to move out of my room and into the attic.

'How is Gran?' I asked, wanting to find out what sort of mood she was in. Gran has two moods: bad and worse. Her bad mood is bearable, she just moans all the time about everything: the government, the council, her neighbours, what's on the telly, or in the papers, or the price of everything. When she's in her worse mood, it's time to watch out. Then she starts picking on people.

'She's feeling well,' said Mum. 'I think she's looking forward to spending time with you and Krystal.'

It was at that moment that we heard a yell from upstairs. It wasn't a yell of pain or fear, it was a scream of … well, disgust, I suppose. It's a sound I've come to recognise. This yell came from Gran, and it was very loud.

Mum glared at me. 'Dave, what have you done?'

'Nothing!' I protested. 'I've only just got home! I haven't even seen Gran!'

'Come on,' said Mum, and she grabbed me and hustled me upstairs.

Gran was standing in the middle of my room, pointing at my chest of drawers with a shaking finger. 'There are things in that chest of drawers!'

Mum gave me an accusing look. 'Well, Dave?'

It's only my Science collection,' I pointed out. 'Things to look at under the microscope.'

'There are creepy crawlies and bugs!' said Gran. 'And tissues with – ' her face took on an expression of disgust, 'muck on them! This room is a health hazard. It needs to be de-contaminated.'

'It's Science!' I protested again.

'It's not, it's disgusting!' said Gran, very fiercely.

Mum gave me one of her serious looks. 'What exactly have you got in that chest of drawers, Dave?'

'Scientific samples,' I explained.

'Insects!' said Gran.

'A few,' I agreed. 'But most of them are dead.'

'What sorts of insects?'

'Fleas, ants, wood lice, spiders, flies, millipedes …,' I started.

Mum stopped me. 'You can get rid of them,' she announced.

I looked at her, horrified. 'But that's my Science collection!'

'Get rid of them,' repeated Mum, even more firmly.

'And the muck!' said Gran.

'That isn't muck,' I insisted. 'It's things like tissue samples.'

'Where did you get tissue samples?' asked Mum suspiciously.

'From the bathroom,' I said. 'They're for my human body Science project. Things like flakes of dandruff I took from Dad's coat. And ear wax. And some pieces of vomit—'

I didn't get the chance to finish listing all the other very important samples I had managed to collect. 'Get rid of them!' said Mum again, even more firmly.

'I feel sick,' said Gran. 'I don't know if I can sleep in this room, knowing the sort of things that have been in here.'

Good, I thought. Maybe you can go in someone

else's room for a change and I won't have to sleep in the attic. But Mum scuppered that by saying, 'Don't worry, Mum, I'll make sure it'll be clean for you.' Then she turned to me and said, 'Let me know as soon as you've got rid of this stuff and I'll come in and disinfect everything.'

With that, Mum and Gran went downstairs, leaving me alone. It was so unfair! It had taken me ages to put this collection together. The drawers were full of small plastic bags with all my carefully collected specimens – vomit I had scraped off a wall, snot from a tissue, a mouse that I'd dissected and put into four separate bags, a dead cockroach, an armpit hair – each one precious.

Well, if they thought I was dumping this collection, they were very much mistaken. I put all my specimens in an old plastic shopping bag and moved them up to the attic, where they would be safe until Gran had gone. Then I filled another old shopping bag with rolled-up newspaper and put it into the dustbin, so they'd think I had thrown everything away.

CHAPTER 13

I did my best to keep out of sight of Gran for the rest of the day. The trouble was, so did Krystal, and so did Dad when he arrived home from work, and then Mum accused us all of avoiding spending time with Gran. Which was true.

Even though I'd instantly regretted telling Sukijeet Patel she could look at our garden pond, I was hoping she would come so I could use it as an excuse to get out of the house. She never turned up, though. I guessed she'd changed her mind, or maybe she'd found a pond to look at nearer her home. Or maybe her dreadful little brother had got in trouble again and they were both in jail.

That evening was much the same as evenings always are when Gran comes to stay with us: Dad keeps finding things to mend so he doesn't have to sit with her in the living room, and Krystal spends all her time in her room. This means that I get grabbed by Mum to 'keep Gran company'. I can't see the point in this because my company doesn't seem to make Gran happy: she just moans about me. Also, I never get a chance to watch what I want on the telly when Gran's around because we have to watch her favourite programmes, and they're rubbish. Programmes about How to Decorate a House, or Famous Illnesses.

I managed to sneak out for a while on the pretext of taking Fred for a walk, but Fred didn't want to go. I think all that walking around for the past couple of days had worn him out, so he just lay inside his tent and refused to get up when I put on his lead. He didn't snarl or anything when I tugged at him to move, just went floppy and wagged his tail, so I gave up.

That night I made up my bed in the attic. It was a camp bed, which wasn't very comfortable: all metal struts that fixed together at funny angles. I was just dropping off to sleep when, CRASH!!! There was a clap of thunder outside. A second later, lightning lit up the whole of the attic, and there was another crash of thunder, and then it began to rain. Great heavy drops thudding down, hitting the roof so hard I thought it was going to fall in on me. I buried myself under my duvet to try to cut out the noise but instead it got worse, and turned into a loud banging. Then I realised this wasn't the rain, it really was a loud banging, on the other side of the door.

I peered out. It was Dad.

'Dave,' he said, 'your dog's howling and stopping Gran from sleeping.'

I was about to say that Fred wasn't my dog, I was only looking after him, but before I got the chance, Dad said, 'You'd better go and sort it out.'

Then he disappeared.

I lay there on my camp bed, listening to the rain hammering down on the roof, and thought, Why me? Let someone else deal with it.

Then Krystal banged my door open. 'Your dog's stopping Gran from sleeping!' she raged. 'Sort it!'

I struggled into my clothes and went downstairs. Gran was on the landing, having a go at Dad because she couldn't get to sleep – as if it was his fault it was raining. As I reached them, she growled at me, 'People shouldn't have dogs if they can't take proper care of them.' Then she went back inside my room. My room, which was warm and dry and didn't have the sound of rain crashing down on it.

As I stepped outside, the sky lit up with another

flash of lightning, followed shortly afterwards by a
huge clap of thunder. Poor Fred had managed to
get his chain caught round the tentpole and was
howling loudly, mixed with barking, trying to
untangle himself from the remains of the tent, which
had collapsed on him. He obviously didn't like the
thunder and lightning and rain any more than I
did.

I unhooked him from his chain and led him
through the back door into the kitchen. He was

shaking with fright, so I stroked him and rubbed his ears and said things like, 'It's all right, Fred,' and, 'Calm down, boy,' until finally he stopped shivering.

Meanwhile, outside, the rain continued.

I thought about what to do. If I put Fred back outside on his chain, he'd likely just start howling again and disturb Gran, and I'd get in trouble. If I left him in the kitchen, he'd fart all night and when everybody came down for breakfast the kitchen would smell like a drain, and again I'd get into trouble. If I stayed outside in the rain with him, I'd get wet, and get in trouble. There was only one answer and that was to take Fred up to the attic and let him stay with me for the night, next to the camp bed. So that's what I did.

Luckily, now that Fred had stopped howling, everyone had gone back to bed, so I was able to sneak him up the stairs and into the attic without being seen. Of course, the first thing Fred did as soon as he got in the attic was let off a fart, so I had to open the window to let the smell out. Then the rain started to come in, so I had to shut the window again.

There was one positive thing, though: it seemed to me that Fred's farts weren't as strong as they had been on that first day. Perhaps the healthier food I was giving him, plus lots of walks, meant he wasn't quite so smelly. Or perhaps my nose was just getting used to it.

CHAPTER 14

Next morning, I woke up to find a sort of green cloud hanging in the attic. As I hurried to open the window, I decided I was wrong about Fred's farts losing their noxious strength. Fred was pleased to see me and wagged his tail, as always, which did help to circulate the odours and drive them towards the fresh air.

I took hold of Fred's collar and hurried him downstairs, hoping to get him outside before anyone realised he'd spent the night in the house. It was just my luck that, as I got to the landing, the door of my room opened and Gran appeared.

She looked at both Fred and me disapprovingly and said, 'I hope that dog's house-trained.'

Just as she spoke, Fred let off a classic silent-but-deadly and Gran staggered back into my room, her eyes crossed as if someone had bashed her over the head. I managed to get Fred outside and back on his chain without anyone else noticing, though. I spent some time mending the tent, and he seemed quite happy in it.

The morning started off as usual. Mum and Dad went to work, Gran moaned, and Krystal tried various dodges to get out of the house (such as claiming she had to spend time with her best friend, Shelly, because Shelly wasn't well). Gran, however, had lots of errands she wanted Krystal to run.

I was getting ready to take Fred for yet another walk when there was a knock at the door. Krystal ran to open it in the hope she could find an excuse to get away from Gran, but she came back looking disappointed.

'It's for you,' she scowled. 'It's your girlfriend.'

'I don't have a girlfriend,' I protested, going to the door.

There was Sukijeet Patel with her little brother,

Anwar. 'Hello,' she said. 'I've come to look at your pond, like you said.'

Glad of the chance to escape from Gran's scowl, I took Sukijeet and Anwar out to our back garden. As I'd told her, the pond wasn't big enough to hold any fish, but it was Dad's pride and joy. To be honest, if aliens from another planet had looked at our garden, they would have assumed there were no such things as flowers or plants, that humans just filled their

gardens with ornaments: garden gnomes and weird sculpture. The pond was the nearest thing to nature; it had real plants growing in it.

'It's great!' Sukijeet said. 'Perfect for my project!' She took some plastic bottles out of the bag she'd brought with her and knelt down beside the pond.

'I thought you were coming round yesterday,' I mentioned. 'You know, after the park.'

Her face fell. 'I couldn't,' she said. 'I was too upset.'

'What, just because of the ranger?' I asked.

'No,' she said. 'That horrible boy from school was there. Bates. With a gang.' At the thought of it, she looked really miserable.

'What happened?' I asked.

'Anwar kicked his football and it hit one of them.'

Good old Anwar! I thought. I hoped it had been Banger Bates he'd hit.

'They came over and started harassing us,' Sukijeet went on. 'They wouldn't give Anwar his ball back. And when I said I was going to call the ranger and make them give it back, they laughed. And then they said they were going to beat us up and throw us into the pond. I only just managed to get Anwar away from them, and run home. It was horrible.'

She fell silent. I felt sorry for her, knowing from first-hand experience how terrifying Banger Bates could be. Add his horrible gang to the mix, and it would have been even worse. What got me was that the park ranger, despite all his muscles, only seemed to throw his weight around when telling off a six-year-old kid like Anwar. When real trouble turned up in the shape of Banger and his gang, the ranger was nowhere to be seen.

'At least you managed to get away,' I said.

'Yes, but where can I go with Anwar now?' she asked. 'The park was the best place for him to have a run around. The streets are too dangerous with all the traffic, and he gets bored when he stays cooped up in our flat.'

'Don't worry,' I said. 'Banger Bates and his gang won't be at the park all the time.'

She sighed. 'I hate it. All I want to do is get on with my Science project.'

'Well, you can,' I said. 'Feel free to do what you want with our pond. In fact, I'll give you a hand. What do you need?'

'I'd like some pondweed,' said Sukijeet.

'No problem.' I picked up one of the plastic bottles.

As we were kneeling down, I heard a noise behind

us and looked round to see Paul standing there. He had come round the back way and was glaring at us, with his schoolbag under his arm.

'Paul!' I said.

'I'm sorry to interrupt,' he said coldly. 'I've brought round my Science project but I see you've got a new friend.'

And with that, he turned and walked off.

I got up. 'No, Paul! Wait—!' I began, and started to hurry after him, but a sudden huge splash made me stop and look round.

Anwar had fallen into the pond.

CHAPTER 15

For a moment, I hesitated. Should I go after Paul and explain what had happened? But before I could make a move, Anwar began to wail. The next thing, pandemonium broke out. Fred began to bark excitedly at the sound of Anwar's wailing, and Gran and Krystal appeared.

'What's going on?' demanded Gran. Then she saw Anwar sitting in the pond, soaking wet and with pondweed hanging down from the top of his head. He looked like one of those creatures you see in fantasy movies.

'What's that in the pond?' she snapped.

'It's my brother,' said Sukijeet.

'Who pushed him in?' demanded Krystal.

'No one!' I said. 'He fell in!'

Sukijeet was now helping Anwar out, being careful not to let him make her wet.

'I fell in the pond,' moaned Anwar, as if we were all idiots who hadn't spotted the fact that he was soaked and covered in pondweed.

All this time, Fred was leaping about and barking and getting excited, which – of course – made him fart. The good thing was, both Gran and Krystal beat a hasty retreat indoors as soon as the smell hit them. The bad thing was that Gran glared at me

and snapped, 'Sort that dog out and then I want to talk to you!' in a threatening manner.

Then she remembered that Anwar was still standing there, dripping wet and about to catch pneumonia, so she gestured at Sukijeet and said, 'You'd better bring him indoors. Krystal, get a towel.'

Krystal opened her mouth to say something like, 'What did your last slave die of?' which is the sort of thing she does, then she remembered she was dealing with Gran, who is so tough she eats people raw, so she went off to do as she was told. Sukijeet took hold of Anwar and took him inside, and Gran followed them all in and shut the door. I was left with the excitedly barking and farting Fred, who looked like he was about to get his chain caught up in my makeshift tent again.

I was just calming Fred down when I heard Dad's voice say, 'Hello? What's going on?'

I turned round, and there he was. For some reason he'd decided to come home in the middle of the day. He looked at the pond, and then took another look, his mouth dropping open.

'Where's all the water from my pond gone?' he asked. 'Has that dog drunk it?'

'No,' I said. 'A little boy fell into it. He's indoors now with Gran and everyone. They're getting him dry.'

Dad gaped. 'My pond?' he said, shocked. 'My best pond?'

I was about to say, 'It's your only pond,' but he looked so shocked I decided to keep my mouth shut.

Dad stumbled over to his pond and looked at it. The water level had gone down a bit, I had to admit, but not by very much. I mean, it wasn't as if a whale had fallen into it and emptied all the water out. Dad stood there, staring in horror.

'I put special pondweed in there just two days ago,' he said. 'Now it's gone!' He turned at looked at me, still stunned. 'First that dog destroys my favourite garden gnome, now some boy comes along and ruins my pond! Why?'

'He didn't do it on purpose,' I said.

'What was he even doing here?' demanded Dad.

I was about to say, 'I told him and his sister they could come and look at the pond,' but decided that would be dropping me in even deeper trouble, so I just muttered, 'I don't know.'

All right, as lies go, it wasn't the best. I nearly added, 'I've never seen him before in my life,' but as Dad would soon meet Anwar in our kitchen being dried off by Gran, and probably find out that I'd invited him and Sukijeet round, such a lie would only make things worse.

Just then the back door opened and Gran appeared.

'Has that dog stopped making smells yet?' she snapped fiercely. Then she saw Dad. 'What are you doing here? Why aren't you at work?'

'I was on a job round the corner, so I thought I'd pop home and make sure everything was all right,' said Dad.

'Well, it isn't,' said Gran. 'That dog keeps making

smells and giving me a headache with its barking. And some boy just fell in the pond so I'm having to clean him up.'

Then she stepped aside, and out came Sukijeet and Anwar. Anwar was wearing some of my clothes! And not just any old clothes, but my very best Science Museum T-shirt!

'He's wearing my Science Museum T-shirt!' I said, shocked.

'He had to put something on,' said Gran. 'He can't walk home dripping wet. Krystal fetched some clothes for him from your room.'

I looked at Krystal, standing behind Gran in the doorway, and saw the nasty smile she gave me. She knew how important to me my Science Museum T-shirt was. Out of all the clothes she could have chosen, she'd given that to Anwar on purpose.

Sukijeet had Anwar's wet clothes in a plastic bag. 'I'm sorry for any trouble we've caused,' she said. 'I'd better take Anwar home. I'll bring the clothes back.'

With that, she put her arm round Anwar and walked off, the carrier bag of his wet clothes in one hand, and the bag with her Science project in hanging from the other.

Dad was still looking stunned, as if the end of the world had come. 'That boy ruined my pond!' he said, pointing at it.

'It was never much of a pond to start with!' snapped Gran. She turned to me and said threateningly, 'Remember, I want a word with you when you've finished sorting that dog out.' Then she went inside.

'It was Dave's fault,' said Krystal. 'If he hadn't brought that dog and those kids round here, none of this would have happened.' She gave me a sly smirk to show that she knew she'd dropped me right in it, and went indoors.

Dad scowled at me. 'Krystal's right,' he said. 'This is all your fault. Well, don't think you're getting that twenty pounds I promised you.'

I gaped at him in shock. This was so unfair!

'Anwar falling in the pond wasn't disgusting!' I

protested. 'You said you wouldn't pay me if I did anything disgusting! This wasn't disgusting. It was an accident, and not my fault!'

Dad stood there, his face going all different shades to show he was angry: white, then purple, then white again. But I knew he couldn't defeat my logic. Also, if he really wasn't going to pay me, then he knew I had nothing to lose so I could be as disgusting as I wanted.

Finally he snapped out, 'All right. But if anything else happens, that's it! You'll get no twenty pounds from me!'

And with that, he stomped inside too.

I stood there, patting Fred to keep him calm and thinking that things couldn't get any worse. As I bent over to untangle his chain from the tent, he farted and got me right in the nose.

CHAPTER 16

The rest of that day was a nightmare. First I got told off by Gran for causing a nuisance. Then I got told off again by Dad for ruining his garden gnome and messing up his pond, and upsetting Gran. And just after that had finished, Mum arrived home from work and was told what had happened by everyone. Then she told me off for upsetting Gran, Dad, Krystal, Fred, and everyone else. In fact, to hear Mum go on at me, you'd have thought I was responsible for everything that had gone wrong in the whole history of the planet, including earthquakes, the plague and global warming. There was no doubt about it, my life was becoming a disaster.

I tried phoning Paul to explain why Sukijeet and her brother had been at my house, but I only got the answering machine with a stupid message from Paul's dad, trying to be funny and pretending he's a famous person. He changes it every month. This month's message went, 'Hello, this is Prince Charles. I'm afraid Edward and Paul Sears can't come to the phone right now, but if you leave a message I'm sure they'll get back to you.' The voice sounded nothing at all like Prince Charles; in fact it was more like a parrot with a blocked nose.

It struck me that maybe Paul was deliberately not answering the phone because he knew it was me (his phone has one of those displays which shows you who's calling). I wanted to put things right, because I felt bad about him coming round and getting the wrong impression about Sukijeet being there. I told Mum and Dad that I had to see Paul, but Mum just flared up.

'You're not going anywhere, young man!' she said. 'You've caused enough trouble in this house, and if you think you can sneak off instead of spending time with your gran, you are very much mistaken.'

'But I will spend time with Gran!' I said. 'I just have to tell Paul something.'

'No!' said Mum firmly. To Dad, she said, 'Tell him, John.'

I looked at Dad, who looked at me and sighed.

'Your mum's right,' he said. 'This might seem hard, but it's the only way you're going to learn. I've obviously been too soft on you. You're staying in to keep Gran company.'

It looked like I was caught. 'OK,' I said, adding

hopefully, 'But I'd better take Fred for a walk so he can do his business.'

'Oh no, you don't!' said Mum sharply. 'Don't think you're using that dog as an excuse to go out. Your dad will take him for his walk. Won't you, John?'

Dad looked doubtful about this at first, but then he nodded.

And so I was stuck indoors with Gran and no way of escape. It was so unfair! None of this was my fault! I thought about going online and checking websites about human rights to see if I could sue anybody for wrongful imprisonment, but there wasn't much point.

I tried phoning Paul's number again, but once again all I got was Paul's dad doing his dreadful Prince Charles impersonation. This time I left a message.

'Hi, Paul. It's Dave. I'm sorry you got the wrong end of the stick when you came round. Sukijeet's not my friend. She just came to our house to look at my dad's pond. I can't come round to yours because

I got in trouble and my parents won't let me out of the house.'

I was going to say more, but decided against it. With my luck, it would only make things worse.

CHAPTER 17

That evening was miserable. I was kept prisoner in the house, banned from going out. Mum agreed that Krystal could stay over at her friend Shelly's house. Dad took Fred for his walk, and then went into the garage to 'do some DIY'. I knew he was just trying to avoid sitting with Gran. When Gran's not with us he spends most of his time in front of the telly; the only time he gets enthusiastic about DIY is when Gran comes to stay. Mum decided there was a programme about Aborigines she wanted to watch. Gran said she wasn't interested in Aborigines, and it showed how poor we were that we could only afford one telly.

'My next-door neighbour's daughter has four television sets in her house!' said Gran. 'It means everyone can watch what they want. It's very civilised.' Then she added, 'But then, she married a man with brains and money.'

'If you ask me, it shows how shallow some people's lives are that they need to have four television sets,' countered Mum. 'They obviously have nothing in common, and they don't want to talk to one another. That sounds like a very unhappy household and makes me even more determined to only ever have one TV.'

Actually, both Krystal and I had asked if we could have TVs in our rooms because neither of us likes watching the same programmes as Dad and Mum, but Mum and Dad had said no, they couldn't afford it.

I thought Mum had been very clever in the way she argued her point, because it shut Gran up. But only for a while. Then Gran said, 'It's a pity that while I'm here you can't make allowances and put on something I like to watch. After all, I'm not here all that often.'

'I know that,' said Mum, 'but I've watched the rest of the series and this is the last programme, so I don't want to miss it.'

With that, she switched on the television. Gran sat in the armchair and sulked for a bit, then she said, 'Well, if I can't watch TV I'll do my knitting wool. Dave can help me.'

Knitting wool? Me?

'I don't know anything about knitting,' I pointed out.

'Then it's about time you learnt,' said Gran. 'You never know when it will come in useful.'

When pigs fly, I thought. But I didn't say that out loud.

'Come on,' said Gran. 'My wool is in the kitchen.'

I followed her into the kitchen, hardly able to believe this was actually happening to me. Knitting! I'd seen people do it and I knew it involved long needles. If there was an accident I could seriously harm myself!

'I don't know how to knit,' I tried again.

'You're not going to find out,' said Gran. 'I need

to wind my wool into balls. All you have to do is sit there with the skein on your hands while I wind it into a ball.'

I looked at her, baffled. 'What's a skein?' I'd never heard the word before.

She shook her head. 'Your parents haven't taught you anything, have they? Sit down and hold out your hands, about a foot apart.'

I sat down and held out my hands. For a moment I thought she was going to thump them, but instead she hooked a long hank of wool over one of my hands and then the other, so it was stretched between them.

Then she took the loose end and begin to wind it into a ball.

'Now don't talk,' she said. 'I need to concentrate.'

And so we sat there in silence. Me holding this long length of wool and Gran winding it up, while in the background we could hear the sound of Aboriginal chants from the TV in the living room, and an occasional drilling and banging from the garage as Dad did something usefully DIY. This was possibly the most boring time I had ever spent on the planet. I could see the minutes stretching into hours, possibly days, with me trapped at the end of a length of wool while Gran turned it into a woolly and my life passed slowly before my eyes.

As I sat there, I started to think about my human body Science project, and how I wished I was spending the time on that instead. At this rate I'd never get it finished and either Paul or Sukijeet would have their project chosen by Miss Moore instead of mine. I was trapped in this weird silence, with nothing to do except look at the wool unravelling from my hands and being turned into a fluffy ball by Gran, and all I could do was stare ahead.

Gran was sitting right in front of me. Suddenly it struck me that her face would be ideal for a section of my Science project. It was perfect! She had the sort of skin that people get when they're really, really old: wrinkly and lumpy, with small brown spots on it here and there. And there were some hairs sticking out of one of her nostrils! I wondered why the hairs were only sticking out of one and not the other. Had she cut the hairs in the other? If so, how did she get the blades of the scissors into her nostril? Did they get covered in snot when she did it? And why did she only cut the hairs in one nostril?

Then I looked at her ears. Sure enough, there were tufts of hair sticking out of one of them! But the hair on top of her head looked to be getting thin. Wow, this was an incredible scientific discovery! As the hair on her head began to disappear, it began to sprout in other places like her ears and nostrils! And

her chin! I noticed that one of the pimples on her chin actually had a hair growing out of it! Was this the beginnings of a beard?

I looked more closely, and spotted a line of hairs growing beneath Gran's nose, above her upper lip. She had a moustache! A moustache and a beard! Was she turning into a man?

Suddenly I realised the wool on my hands had

stopped moving, and I became aware of Gran glaring at me, looking very suspicious. 'What are you staring at?' she demanded.

I couldn't help myself; I had to know for the sake of my project. 'Why have you only got hairs growing out of one of your nostrils?' I asked.

The effect was amazing. It was as if I'd stuck a pin in her bottom. She sprang to her feet and stared at me, and then she said, 'You disgusting boy!'

She dropped the ball of wool on the chair and went out to the living room, calling, 'Sandra! Your son has insulted me!'

I was shocked by this. I hadn't insulted her at all, I was just curious on a scientific level. Then I heard

Gran call out again, 'Sandra! Where are you?'

Mum appeared from outside, looking worried. 'Has anyone seen the dog?' she asked.

Gran and I looked at her, puzzled.

'No,' we said.

'Why?' Gran asked.

'I thought I heard a noise so I went outside, and the dog's gone. He's vanished!'

CHAPTER 18

Gran and I followed Mum out into the garden, and sure enough, there was Fred's chain, but no Fred. He had definitely gone.

'How did he get off the chain?' asked Mum, baffled.

She vanished inside the house, and a few minutes later the sound of drilling and banging from the garage stopped and she reappeared with Dad, who also looked at the empty chain with a baffled expression.

'Where's he gone?' he asked.

'That's what we want to know,' said Mum.

'I expect you didn't put him back on the chain properly when you brought him back from his walk,' Gran remarked sniffily.

'Yes, I did!' protested Dad. 'I'm not useless, you know!'

Gran stayed silent, but gave him one of her looks that said, 'Oh yes, you are.'

I went to the chain and examined the end. It wasn't broken, so either Fred had managed to slip out of it in some way, or someone had come along and unhooked him from the chain.

'He's been stolen,' I said.

'Nonsense!' said Gran. 'Who'd steal a dog that makes those awful smells?'

'They wouldn't know he makes bad smells at first,' said Mum. 'They'd see him on the chain and just think, There's a dog!' She looked really unhappy. 'That must have been the noise I heard, someone stealing him. We should never have let him stay outside the house where anyone could see him!'

'He was at the back of the house,' pointed out Dad. 'No one could have seen him unless they came round the back.'

'And that's exactly what these people do!' said Mum.

'What people?'

'Criminals. Crooks. Burglars. Dognappers!'

Slowly the awful impact of this whole thing sank in for me. Fred had been stolen! Banger Bates's gran's dog! When Banger found out, my life would be over. I'd have to leave the country, or go into hiding until I was old enough to grow a beard and change my name.

'But why would anyone want to steal a dog?' persisted Dad.

'For their fur,' said Gran. 'I read about it in the paper. People steal dogs and sell their fur to make coats.'

Mum began to look even unhappier at this thought. 'Poor Fred!' she moaned.

'In some countries they eat dogs,' added Gran. 'It was in the paper. And I saw a TV programme about it.'

I looked at her in horror. 'They eat dogs?' I echoed, shocked.

Gran nodded. 'For them it's no different to us eating a cow or a lamb. They eat dogs instead.'

Oh no! Poor Fred! Turned into a stew, or carved up and served up on a plate.

'But no one in this country eats dogs,' Dad pointed out.

'Maybe they steal them here and then ship them out to countries that do,' said Gran. 'After all, we send beef and lamb abroad for other people to eat.'

I wondered how I was going to explain this to Banger Bates, and realised I couldn't. My only

chance was to say that Fred was dead, that he'd been run over or something. The more I thought about it, the sadder I felt. Poor Fred. I had really grown to like the dog, and the thought of him being stolen and being turned into a pie … It was just too horrible.

'We have to call the police,' said Mum. 'The dognappers can't have got far.'

'I didn't hear anything,' said Dad.

'I'm not surprised, with the noise you were making,' said Mum. 'All that drilling and banging. If you hadn't been making such a racket we could have saved the dog! We'd have heard the thieves when they crept round and unhooked him from his chain.'

With that she went inside, grabbed the phone and began to dial 999. Gran and Dad followed her. As I heard her say, 'Police? I want to report a stolen dog!' I looked at the end of Fred's chain, and a feeling of great sadness came over me.

CHAPTER 19

The police arrived about two hours after Mum phoned, which made her mad. 'The crooks could have got anywhere by now!' she fumed while we waited.

'The police can't just turn up immediately,' Dad pointed out. 'They could be miles away. Or on another case.'

There were two of them, both in uniform, a man and a woman. I was disappointed, having hoped that at least one of them would be a detective. What also disappointed me was the fact they didn't do any of the things you see the police do on TV. On TV, they put tape all over the place to seal off the crime scene, take fingerprints and impressions of footprints and tyres, bring in a forensic team, and put up a big

white tent to stop evidence being ruined.

This pair just asked questions and scribbled the answers down in a notebook. Most of the questions were pretty straightforward: name, address of property, description of dog. It was when they asked if the dog was ours that things got tricky.

'No,' said Mum. 'Our son, Dave, has been looking after it for an old lady.'

The man police officer with the notebook held his

pen ready and asked, 'And the name and address of this old lady?'

My heart sank. The awful truth was going to come out. The next thing would be the police going round to Banger Bates's house and telling him that Fred had gone, and then he'd come round here and tear my head off.

'She's in hospital,' said Mum.

'Oh?' said the woman police officer. 'Which hospital?'

'I don't know,' said Mum, and she turned to me. 'Which hospital is it?'

I was aware of all of them looking at me, and I felt myself breaking out into a sweat. 'I can't remember. It was her family who were looking after the dog.'

As I realised the next question they were going to ask: What's the name and address of her family? I felt myself go cold with fear. This was it. There was no escaping my fate. I was doomed! Then, like a miracle, Fate intervened in the wonderful, magical form of Mum.

'He's in shock,' she said out of the side of her mouth, nodding towards me.

The man police officer nodded and snapped his notebook shut. 'Understood,' he said. 'We'll put out an alert for the dog.'

'Aren't you going to check for footprints?' I asked. 'The dognappers might have left tracks in the garden. They must have been on foot because Dad said he didn't hear a vehicle.'

'Yes, but I was busy in the garage,' said Dad.

The two police officers nodded sympathetically at him.

'Don't worry, sir, it wasn't your fault,' said the woman. To me, she said, 'Trust us, son. We'll do our best. We know the sort of people who do this sort of thing. We'll go and check them out. If this dog can be found, we'll find it.'

And with that, they left.

By this time it was getting late, and Mum suggested I ought to get to bed and get some rest. Normally I'd find every excuse to stay up, but what with Gran blighting the house like some monster, and feeling the way I did about Fred, I just nodded and said goodnight, and went up to the attic.

I lay in bed, feeling really miserable. Not just because Banger Bates was going to beat me up, but because of poor Fred. It was strange: I'd never been interested in having a pet before. Fred was the first animal I'd looked after, and I'd become very fond of him in such a short time. OK, he farted, but then so did lots of people. Our next-door neighbour, Mr Biddiwick, farted, but no one put him on a chain in the back yard.

Poor old Fred. I remembered the way he looked at me with those big soft eyes, and the way he pushed his wet nose into my hand when he was being friendly. And it wasn't a snotty wet nose, either, it was a friendly wet nose. In fact, more damp than actually wet.

I wondered where he was. My hope was that he hadn't been stolen after all but had managed to get free of the chain somehow and run away. If that was the case, there was a chance he might come back. If he'd been stolen, there was no chance. All sorts of horrible things might happen to him. He could be sold to one of those laboratories where they test drugs and chemicals on animals, and make them smoke cigarettes, or try out new experimental medicines on them. I read in one of my science magazines that they use rabbits to test shampoo because rabbits don't have tear ducts and so can't blink and get the shampoo out of their eyes.

Or, as Gran said, Fred could be turned into food. Or his fur sold to make a coat. And for either of

those two things to happen, Fred would have to be dead; I felt so bad about that, I almost started to cry. But then I bit my lip and told myself not to be so soft. He was only a dog. And someone else's dog as well. But the truth was, he was a lovely good-natured dog and I had become really fond of him.

I felt so guilty. It was my fault he had been left outside on a chain where people could steal him. I should have insisted he come inside. He could have stayed in my room. Okay, he farted, but farts were natural.

As I lay there, feeling guilty and sad and miserable, I heard Gran clumping up the stairs and calling back down to my mum and dad in a grumpy tone. I heard my name, and realised she'd finally remembered to moan to them about me mentioning the hairs in her nose. I sighed. I was in for it tomorrow.

Then I heard the door of my room open, followed by a thud. Not just a little thud, but a really heavy thud of something falling to the floor. It was so heavy that the whole house shook, and for a moment I thought we'd suffered an earthquake. In fact, not many people know this but we have earthquakes in Britain more often than people think. According to my science magazines, some of them score quite high on the Richter Scale, which is how earthquakes are measured.

I was just thinking these thoughts when I heard Mum call out, 'Mum?' in a worried tone of voice, and knew that something awful had happened. That thud was obviously something to do with Gran. Had she fainted? Or had something even worse happened to her? It was starting to seem as if bad luck was hanging over our house: first Fred is stolen and turned into meat pies, and then Gran....

I heard Mum's footsteps hurrying up the stairs, then she screamed and yelled out 'John!' in panic, and I knew something really bad had happened.

I should have stayed there in bed and pretended to be asleep, but the scientist in me wanted to find out what it was. And, if Gran had fallen down dead, I wondered what she looked like.

I hurried down from the attic just as Dad started up the stairs. Mum was standing in the door of my room; her face was white and she looked shocked. I could see Gran's slippered feet poking out of the doorway, and they weren't moving. There was another thing as well: a really bad smell. I had heard that people's bodies rotted and smelt awful when they died, but I didn't think it happened so quickly. Holding my nose, I got to the door of my room just as Dad reached the landing.

The bad smell wasn't coming from Gran. Fred was standing in the middle of my room, a smile on his face and his tail wagging. And on the carpet was a very large pile of steaming poo.

Gran began to twitch. I heard her moan, 'The dog …'

Then Fred went to her and began to lick her face.

That did it: Gran woke up completely. She let out a scream as Fred's tongue washed her cheek and

she rolled backwards out of the doorway, nearly knocking Mum and Dad over.

She struggled to sit up and pointed into my room. 'Can you smell it?' she demanded, her voice shaking. 'That dog has been stuck in my room, farting. And he's done a … a thing in the middle of the carpet!'

FACTOID:
Poo
The brown colour of poo comes from a chemical called bilirubin. Bilirubin is made from old red blood cells. Bilirubin is rich in iron, which is why it makes poo that colour.

'That's because he was trapped,' I said, on Fred's behalf. After all, it wasn't Fred's fault, he couldn't open the door and get to the bathroom.

Gran and Mum ignored me. They were both too intent on blaming Dad.

'This is your fault, John!' Mum told him angrily. 'You obviously didn't put him on the chain securely enough, and he got off and came indoors and managed somehow to get into Mum's room.'

My room, I corrected them silently. Fred got into my room. And he only farted because he was worried about being trapped there. And as for doing the poo … well, the steam rising from it showed it was pretty recent, so he'd kept it in for as long as he could.

'It wasn't my fault!' protested Dad. 'Someone must have let him off the chain!'

And they all turned and looked accusingly at me.

'It wasn't me!' I protested. 'I didn't see Fred the whole evening.'

'Don't try and put the blame on Dave!' said Mum. 'It was your fault!' Then a horrifying thought struck her, and she put her hand to her mouth. 'Oh no! We reported him to the police as being stolen! They'll charge us with wasting police time.'

'Serves you right,' snapped Gran. She gestured into my room. 'Well, I'm not sleeping in there tonight. Not with that smell, and that … that pile of doings! I shall sleep in Krystal's room tonight. And tomorrow I shall go home! I will not stay another day in this house until that dog has gone!'

And she stormed off into Krystal's room and slammed the door shut.

Fred had now come out on the landing and was pushing his damp nose against me and wagging his tail, happy to be free.

'I'll go and put him on his chain,' I said.

'And I'll go and phone the police and tell them everything's all right,' said Mum. 'I'll say he managed to find his way home.'

Which, in a way, was true. Fred had managed to find my room.

As I led Fred downstairs, Dad stopped me. 'When you've tied him up, you can clean up that mess in the room,' he said sternly, adding, 'After all, it's your fault the dog came here in the first place.'

OK, it was unfair of Dad to expect me to clean up the poo, when it was really his fault Fred had escaped from the chain and got into my room.

But at that moment it didn't matter to me. What mattered was that Fred was safe. He hadn't been stolen and turned into meat, or part of a fur coat, or sold for animal experiments. He was still the same happy farting dog as before.

And I was pretty sure Fred's farts weren't as bad as before. If they had been, none of us would have been able to stand on the landing, talking. No, without a doubt, Fred's farts were no longer as potent.

CHAPTER 20

The next morning, I crept downstairs early and took Fred for a walk so he could do his business. I didn't want him leaving piles of poo over Dad's precious garden, otherwise I'd get in even worse trouble and bang would go the twenty pounds he'd promised me.

When we got back, I put Fred on his chain, making sure he couldn't escape this time, and headed for the house. Dad came out as I went in. He was carrying Gran's suitcase.

'Your gran's going home, and it's all your fault!' he said crossly. Then he lugged her suitcase to the car.

I was shocked. For Dad to blame me when it was his fault that Fred had got into my room was so unfair.

And also, Dad had been the first one to complain when he found out Gran was coming to stay with us! You'd have thought he'd have given me a friendly pat on the head and a ten-pound note to celebrate, instead of telling me off.

I went into the kitchen warily, keeping a watchful eye out for Gran, but she was nowhere to be seen. 'Where's Gran?' I asked.

'She's upstairs,' said Mum. 'Packing.'

I marvelled at how much luggage my gran dragged around with her when she came to stay. Dad had already hauled one massive suitcase out to the car, and yet she still had enough stuff left to fill another one! I dreaded to think what she'd need to take with her if she went somewhere really far away, and for a long time. Enough cases to fill a cargo ship, I expect.

I took the packet of cereal to shake myself some into a bowl, just as Krystal arrived home. She looked like she hadn't slept at all, and my guess was she hadn't. I think when she says she's staying round at

Shelly's house they secretly go to wild parties. One day I'm going to crack the combination lock on her diary and find out what really goes on.

Krystal put down her bag and looked around. 'Where's Gran?' she asked.

'In your room,' said Mum.

'My room?!' said Krystal, puzzled.

'Yes,' said Mum. 'She slept there last night.' And then she left to go and see Gran.

For a second, Krystal stood there in a state of shock as this horrifying thought sunk in: Gran had actually slept in her bed and used her things. The next second, she had grabbed me and pulled my head back, until I thought my hair was going to come out by the roots.

FACTOID:
Hair
Human beings have the same number of hairs on their bodies as chimpanzees.

'This is your fault!' she snarled. 'What did you do to make her sleep in my room with all those disgusting Granny smells? Yurk!'

'Nothing?' I gasped, adding 'Ow!' as she tightened her grip on my hair.

'Then why is she in there?'

'She's packing to go home.'

Krystal let go and looked at me, bewildered. 'She's going home?'

'Yes,' I said, nodding, but not too hard. My scalp still felt fragile from where Krystal had grabbed hold of it.

Suddenly she smiled. 'This is your fault, isn't it?' she said. I was about to deny it strongly, before I realised her smile was genuine, she was feeling good. 'You did something really disgusting and it's driven Gran out!'

'Well …' I began modestly.

To my surprise, Krystal leant forward and kissed me on the top of my head. 'You are a wonderful brother!' she said delightedly. Then her expression

changed and she pointed a finger threateningly at me. 'But if you tell anyone I said so, I will kill you.'

'I won't say a word,' I promised.

There was a thumping sound from upstairs and Gran appeared, followed by Mum carrying her smaller case.

Gran stood in the kitchen and glared at us. 'I'm sorry I shan't be staying to look after you, Krystal,' she announced sternly, 'but I have been driven out of this house by one of the most disgusting things I have ever experienced.' And she swept out to Dad and the car, Mum following.

Krystal gave me a huge grin. 'I knew it!' she chuckled. 'It was you! Brilliant! I owe you one!'

Then she checked herself, realising she might have overdone the enthusiasm. 'Only you can't claim it,' she added firmly.

'Fair enough,' I said.

We went outside to wave Gran goodbye. She didn't wave back, just sat there in the passenger seat like a block of stone and behaved as if we weren't there.

As the car disappeared along the road, I heaved a sigh of relief. No more sleeping in the attic. I had my own room back.

CHAPTER 21

Once Gran had gone, I decided to take Fred out for a walk. There were two reasons for doing this: one, I could call on Paul while I was out and two, although I was in Krystal's good books at the moment, experience told me that her good mood would soon wear off and she'd be back to the anti-Dave terrifying monster she usually was.

I tried phoning Paul to tell him I'd be calling round, but once again all I got was his dad's answering machine. This time he'd changed the message from the fake Prince Charles to a man who kept snarling in a terrible American accent, 'You talking to me? You talking to me?' before saying, 'In that case, speak after the beep.'

I hung up without leaving a message. It struck

me that Paul's dad had finally gone over the edge of sanity. I hadn't the faintest idea who the voice on the answerphone message was meant to be. This strange voice made 'Prince Charles' sound almost sensible.

I wondered where Paul was. Maybe he and his dad had gone away for a few days; after all, it was the half-term holiday. I decided to go to the park first with Fred and give him a chance to run around, and call at Paul's house on the way back. Then, after that, I would finally settle down and do some work on my Science project. It was now Thursday and I only had a couple of days left to get it right.

Fred seemed delighted that it was me taking him for a walk, instead of Dad. All the way to the park, I kept a careful eye out in case Banger Bates and his gang were around. I knew they would still be after me over that business with the dog poo in the sweets bag.

When I got there, the first people I saw were Sukijeet and her little brother. They were standing beside the fence that roped off the pond, and Sukijeet was holding a net on a long bamboo pole, poking it at the edge of the pond. By her feet were two jars.

'Hello,' I said. 'Fishing?'

'It's the boy who smells!' chuckled Anwar.

'That wasn't me, that was the dog!' I reminded him.

FACTOID:
Smells
A polar bear can smell a dead seal 20km away.

Sukijeet pulled out the bamboo pole. 'Hello,' she said awkwardly. 'I'm sorry about what happened. You know, Anwar and your pond.'

'That's all right,' I said, even though it wasn't. Anwar had got me into big trouble, but it wasn't her fault.

'What are you doing?'

She looked shamefaced. 'After what happened, I

didn't feel I could come back to your house again,' she explained awkwardly, 'so I decided to try and get some samples from the pond here.'

She held up the net and the bamboo pole. 'I fixed two bamboo canes together to make a really long rod so I could reach the edge of the pond, but it's still really difficult.'

'You could climb over the fence,' I suggested.

'But that would be wrong,' she said, pointing to

the notice that said the pond was shut. 'And what could I do with Anwar? If I took him over the fence with me he might fall in. And that pond is much deeper than your pond. It's dangerous.'

'We could throw you in,' said a voice behind us.

We all turned, to find ourselves looking at Banger Bates and his three mates, Jax, Mick and Pod. They had obviously crept up behind us, and now they stood there, dangerous and nasty smiles on their faces.

Banger laughed. 'Look who it is. The kid who played that dog-mess gag on us. And the little kid who kicked me with the football. And his stupid sister. Well, well. Looks like we get to have our revenge.'

Although I stood there, upright, my legs felt as if they were going to give way. This was truly terrifying! Banger Bates and his mates were in no mood to be talked round, and they had surrounded us to make sure we couldn't make a run for it. We were trapped on one side by the fence around the pond, and on the other by Banger and his gang. I could feel myself swaying, as if I was going to faint.

'What shall we do with 'em, mates?' grinned Banger evilly.

'Chuck 'em in the pond, like you said, Banger!' said Jax.

'But Anwar can't swim!' cried out Sukijeet. She looked as terrified as I felt.

'Then this is a good way for him to learn,' said Banger. 'Come on, lads. Grab 'em!'

And the four of them stepped towards us, hands outstretched.

CHAPTER 22

'Leave them alone!'

The voice came from behind Banger and his mates, and they turned in surprise. It was Paul! He gave Banger a fierce glare and said, 'Dave's my friend. I won't let you hurt him.'

There was a stunned silence, and then Banger laughed. 'Run away, Sears, or you'll get it as well. Go on, get lost. I'll deal with you later.'

'You can deal with me now,' said Paul defiantly, and he came and stood next to me.

I looked at him helplessly. He was putting himself in serious danger because he was my friend, and I felt really bad about it.

'Go Paul,' I whispered to him. 'This isn't your problem. I appreciate what you're doing. It's the bravest thing I've ever known. But I don't want you getting hurt.'

Banger shrugged. 'Well, it looks like the nerd wants to get beaten up and slung in the pond as well,' he said with a smirk. 'That's fine by me.'

He moved towards us, the fingers of his huge hands clenched like claws and a nasty scowl on his face. Behind him, his three mates moved forward as well, spreading out and cutting off any chance we had of running for it.

And then a most amazing thing happened.

Fred growled.

No, that word doesn't do justice to the sound Fred made, which was so much more than a growl. It started somewhere deep down inside and sounded like the hum of a swarm of angry bees, gradually getting louder, and then it swelled to a low menacing rumble that seemed to shake the park.

FACTOID:
Stomach Rumbles
The acids in a human stomach's digestive juices are so powerful, they can dissolve metal.

The four thugs stopped.

'What was that?' asked Pod, puzzled.

They looked around, worried.

Banger chuckled. 'It's the stupid dog!' he laughed. 'He's farting!'

'It didn't sound like a fart,' said Mick nervously. 'It sounded like he was growling.'

'Nah! That dog's never growled in his life!' sneered Banger. 'Now, let's get on with it. Beat 'em up and throw 'em in the pond.'

As the four of them moved towards us, Fred growled again, only louder this time, and now he bared his teeth. For the first time I realised how big and sharp Fred's teeth looked when you saw them up close.

Jax, Mick and Pod stopped again, exchanging worried looks.

'He's definitely growling,' said Mick. 'In fact he looks like he's going to bite us.'

Banger stared at Fred, the dog's teeth bared and that growling noise still rumbling up from his throat, and then he said to his mates, 'This is mad! That dog's soft as anything! Go on, Jax. Walk towards him. He'll soon get out of the way.'

Jax looked panicky. 'Why me?' he demanded. 'He could have gone mad. He could have rabies.'

'Rabies!' snorted Banger. 'I tell you, he's just a soft dog! This idiot's done something to him, that's what's happened!'

'No, you've done something to him, Banger,' I said. 'You were rotten to him, and he hasn't forgotten. Now Fred knows what it's like to be treated with respect and kindness by someone other than your gran, and he knows he doesn't have to put up with you and your sort ever again.'

Jax, Mick and Pod stood there, nervously shooting looks from the growling dog to Banger. Banger stood there like someone trapped. If he just walked off he knew he'd lose face, but if he tried to carry out his threat to beat us up there was a chance Fred would go for him.

If he'd been the slightest bit intelligent, Banger

would have just sneered and walked off with a quick threat. Something like, 'None of you are worth it. I'll see you all on your own later.' But Banger wasn't at all intelligent. As I've said before, he had about one poor brain cell and it was already overworked. He was the sort of bully who hates to lose face in front of anyone, especially his mates, and even more especially his victims.

He looked at Fred, who'd stopped growling now, and then gave a huge scowl.

'I'll show you what this dog is going to put up with!' he snarled. He picked up a branch that had fallen off a tree, and before any of us knew what was happening, he'd swung it hard at Fred.

Fred moved faster than I thought he could. As the branch came down, he leapt at it and grabbed it between his jaws, and then tore it out of Banger's grasp. Then he dropped the branch and leapt at Banger, making a noise that was a mixture of barking and growling, and this time there was no mistaking his feelings.

Banger jumped back so fast, he tripped over his own feet and fell on the grass, and Fred leapt on top of him. It was all I could do to hang on to the lead and pull him off Banger. 'Fred!' I shouted. 'Stop! You'll kill him!'

But Fred carried on growling and barking at Banger sitting on the grass, looking shocked.

I said to Banger's three mates, who were looking

at the scene in shock, 'I can't hold on to him!'

Jax, Mick and Pod turned and saw me clinging to the end of Fred's lead, and their faces went pale.

'My fingers are going numb,' I added.

That did it. The three of them yelled in panic and set off across the park towards the main gate as if a Hound of Hell were after them. Which, in a way, it was.

Fred lunged towards Banger, who threw himself backwards, his mouth open in terror, and then he scrambled to his feet and ran after his mates. In all the years I'd known Banger, I'd never seen him move so fast.

As the four thugs disappeared, Fred calmed down. Anwar looked at him nervously. 'Is he going to bite us?' he asked.

'No,' I said. 'He knows we're his friends.'

I knelt down beside Fred, put my arms round his neck and gave him a big hug. The growling in his throat stopped altogether, and his tail started to wag.

'Thanks, Fred,' I said.

Fred looked at me and his big tongue lolled out of his mouth in a soppy grin. He nuzzled his head against my chest. Then Sukijeeet began to rub Fred's ears and Paul joined in, patting him all over. Finally Anwar stroked the top of Fred's head.

Fred looked at us all with happiness written all over his face. And then he farted. But, hey, he'd just saved us! For that, we'd forgive him anything.

CHAPTER 23

Sukijeet was eager to get Anwar home in case Banger and his gang came back to the park and started bullying them again. After they'd gone, Paul and I sat down on a bench and watched Fred amble round, sniffing happily.

'I called round at your house and your mum told me you'd taken Fred to the park,' said Paul.

'I tried phoning you but I didn't leave a message,' I said. Curious, I asked him, 'Who's your dad meant to be on the latest answering machine message? The strange American who keeps saying, "You talking to me?"'

Paul looked embarrassed. 'He's supposed to be Robert De Niro, the actor. That's what De Niro says in this film, *Taxi Driver*.'

'Why does he keep saying that?' I asked, puzzled.

'No idea,' shrugged Paul. 'I don't understand half of the old films my dad likes. They're really weird.'

We sat there for a moment, both of us relishing the memory of the sight of Banger Bates and his gang running away.

'We saw off Banger Bates and his gang,' smiled Paul. 'You and me. Heroes.'

'You were the hero,' I said. 'I wouldn't have come over the way you did if I'd been in your shoes.'

'Yes, you would,' said Paul.

'No, I'd have been too scared.'

'You would have,' insisted Paul. 'Anyway, I was scared.' He looked at Fred.

'But thanks to Fred, everything turned out all right.'

Fred obviously heard his name, because he looked towards us and began to wag his tail.

'He's a great dog,' Paul said.

'He certainly is,' I agreed.

For the next couple of days, everything seemed to be great. Gran was no longer in our house to moan at me. Dad and Mum left me alone. In between working on my Science project, Paul and I took Fred to the park, and even though I saw Banger Bates and his mates, they turned round and left as soon as they caught sight of me and Paul and Fred. The only dud thing that happened was Krystal shouting at me when I came into the house with a dead frog I'd found by the pond, but that just made me feel everything had returned to normal. Or nearly normal. There was one very sad thing left to do, and that was to take Fred back to Banger's gran at the end of the week.

As I was having breakfast on Friday, I told Mum, 'I've got to take Fred back today.'

'Oh, is the old lady out of hospital?' she asked.

I didn't say anything, just nodded, which wasn't really a lie. Although I suppose it was.

Mum sighed. 'You know, I'll miss him. He seems to have settled down.'

'He's smelly,' said Krystal, munching at a piece of toast. 'The sooner he's gone, the better.'

'He's not as smelly as he used to be,' I said. 'I've sorted out a diet for him. You see, flatulence is caused by a blockage in the intestines which creates a build up of gas—'

Factoid:
Stomach Digestion
It takes about nine seconds for food to get from your mouth to your stomach.
It then takes about seven hours for your stomach to digest the food. That digested food then takes about another five hours to work its way along the small intestine to the large intestine.

'Yuk!' grimaced Krystal, throwing down her half-eaten piece of toast and looking like she was about to be sick. 'You are the most disgusting person ever, ever, ever!'

After breakfast I went out and clipped on Fred's lead, and he wagged his tail. I guessed he was thinking that he was going off to the park again. He'd got used to going there for a morning run.

'Sorry, Fred,' I said. 'It's not the park today. You're going home. Where you belong.'

Even as I said it, I felt sad. A part of me felt that he belonged here, with me. But I knew his real home was with Banger's gran. As I walked him along the street, I wondered what sort of person she was. It was hard to think of people as terrifying as Banger and his dad being part of the same family as some sweet old lady. But then, Krystal and I are part of the same family, and look how horrible Krystal is.

Banger's gran lived on another part of the Grove Farm estate, but her house and the close it was on were completely different from Banger's. She had flowers growing in her front garden, and tubs of plants. In fact the whole close looked like it had been lifted out of a country village and put down in this big estate.

I rang the bell, and when the door opened, this little old white-haired lady stood looking out at me

from behind the security chain. 'Yes?' she said.

And then she saw Fred, and her face lit up. 'Fred!' she said, and took the security chain off.

Fred's tail was wagging so hard I thought he'd knock himself over. He jumped forward and nuzzled himself against her, and she bent down, put her arms around his neck and hugged him.

'It's lovely to see you, Fred!' she said. Then, still patting him, she looked at me and said, 'You must be the boy Edward told me had offered to look after Fred for me.'

'Yes,' I said. 'That's me. My name's Dave Dickens.'

'I hope he hasn't been too much bother,' she said.

I thought of all the things that had happened since I'd picked Fred up the week before: Dad's damaged garden gnome, the lies I'd had to tell Mum, the fact that looking after Fred meant I hadn't been able to get on with my Science project; but most of all the effects of the incredible smells Fred made when he first came to stay, and whether I now had any hope of winning twenty pounds from Dad.

'No,' I said. 'He's been no bother at all. In fact, I've really enjoyed looking after him.'

'I'm so glad,' said Banger's gran. 'I know Edward's been very busy catching up with his school work, which is why he wasn't able to look after Fred himself.'

I looked at her to see if she was smiling as she said this, but she seemed perfectly serious. How anyone could believe such obvious twaddle was beyond me, but then some people can never think anything bad of their own family. Even if they caught their brother standing with a bloodstained axe over a dead body, they'd believe him if he said, 'Someone just pushed this axe into my hands,' just because he's family. (Clearly this would not apply to Krystal.)

'Right,' Banger's gran said. 'I'll go and get some money. How much do I owe you for looking after Fred?'

And this is where I did an incredibly unusual thing. Instead of taking this great opportunity and saying something like, 'Well, my rates for looking after a

dog are 50p an hour. So, 24 hours works out at £12 a day, so for a whole week … ' etc etc, I said, 'No, that's all right. You don't owe me anything. It's been my pleasure.'

And it was. I had enjoyed being with Fred. And, much as I hated Banger Bates, I couldn't take money from this sweet old lady. That's another thing I thought was so unfair: how come Banger had a great gran like this one, while mine was so terrifying? I wondered if our grans could somehow have got swapped, and this nice woman was actually my real gran, and my horrible gran actually belonged to Banger.

'That is so nice of you, young man,' said Banger's gran. She patted Fred again. 'And I have to say, Fred looks very happy. I think he's enjoyed being looked after by you.'

As if he understood what she'd just said, Fred pushed his head against me and carried on wagging his tail. 'See!' said Banger's gran delightedly. 'He does like you!'

'Actually,' I said, 'there is one thing you can do.' I pulled a sheet of paper from my pocket on which I'd written a diet for Fred: a list of the foods he should eat, and those he shouldn't.

Factoid:
Farts
Beans make people fart because they contain sugars that people can't digest. Other foods that cause farting are cauliflower, cabbage, milk, eggs, corn and raisins.

'You know Fred has a problem with making smells?' I began.

'Does he?' said Banger's gran. She shook her head. 'People have mentioned it, but I've never noticed it myself.'

'Well, he does,' I said. 'Or, rather, he did have. So I've made up a list of foods which will help stop him making bad smells.'

She took the list and studied it. 'What a wonderful young man you are! I must admit, a lot of my friends and neighbours don't call on me as often as I'd like, and one or two of them have mentioned it's due to Fred's smells, but, as I said, because I don't notice them, I didn't know what to do about it.'

'Another thing that will help is taking Fred for regular walks,' I said.

Banger's gran sighed. 'Yes,' she said unhappily. 'I used to do that all the time. But since my arthritis has got worse …'

'Well, maybe there's someone else who can take

him for walks for you,' I suggested. 'Like, me, for example.'

She gave me a lovely smile of surprise. 'You?'

'Yes,' I nodded. 'I could come over after school and take him out for a walk. Not every day, of course,' I added hastily. 'But now and then.'

'That would be lovely!' she said. 'Wouldn't it, Fred?'

And she tickled him behind his ears. Fred got even more excited at this and wagged his tail so furiously I was convinced he was going to take off like a helicopter. And then, true to form, he farted: one last nice smelly one.

'Great!' I said. 'Then I'll see you both again. Say, one day next week after school.'

CHAPTER 24

After I left Banger's gran's house, I went round to Banger's. As I walked, I thought how great it was to see Fred so happy. And how strange it was that Banger's gran, who had no sense of smell, grew such beautiful-smelling flowers by her front door.

There was a knot of fear in my stomach as I approached Banger's house. He wouldn't like what I was going to say, and there was a good chance he'd beat me up before I could finish. But I had to say it, otherwise I'd never get any peace inside my head.

Banger was in his front garden, smashing up a child's tricycle with a hammer. He stopped when he saw me and scowled. 'You!' he snarled.

'Yes,' I said. 'I've just taken Fred to your gran's.'

'Yeah,' sneered Banger, flexing his hammer arm at me. 'And now you haven't got that mangy mutt to protect you, I'm going to sort you out, Dickens. You and that girl and her brother, and your nerd mate, Sears.'

'I wouldn't do that if I were you,' I warned him.

'Oh yeah! Why not?'

'Because your gran says I can take Fred out for walks any time I like. And if you touch me, or Paul, or Suki or Anwar, I'm going to walk him right round here and let him tear you to pieces. Think about that.'

With that, I turned and walked away. My heart was thumping with fear as I waited for Banger to come running after me and beat me up. But he didn't, and I felt the fear turn to relief, and then pride. I'd stood up to Banger Bates. Without Fred being with me!

And that's the end of the story. Or, almost the end.

The next week I went back to school with my human body Science project all finished. It was brilliant! It had so many facts that explained everything there was to know about people's insides.

It was far better than Paul's project on the planets. And, as for Sukijeet's project on pond life, well, that was just pictures of plants that grew in water and little insects. All right, some of the insects were interesting, but the rest was boring. And yet it was Sukijeet's project that was chosen by Miss Moore and Miss Nelson for the competition! How mad is that? How unfair!

What was even more unfair was the question of the money Dad had promised me. Twenty pounds if I didn't do anything disgusting for a week, that was the deal. Yet when the time came for him to pay out, he claimed I hadn't kept my side of the bargain. He said that Fred's poo in my room was one of the most disgusting things he'd ever seen. What a cheat! I pointed out to him that the whole thing was his fault because if he'd put Fred on the chain securely, Fred would never have got into my room in the first place. Dad then started talking about the disgusting smells Fred made when he farted. I argued that it was the dog who'd been disgusting, not me, but Dad said that I'd been the one who'd brought Fred to the house, so it came down to me. And I didn't get the twenty pounds.

In my view, Dad had cheated me out of my money, and I wondered if I could sue him for breach of contract. But then I thought, if I did, it would only make things worse. That's the problem with being a kid. The adults are powerful just because they're bigger and richer than you. But one day I'll get my own back. When I'm a famous scientist earning zillions of pounds through my discoveries and inventions, I shall invent a really bad smell which only knocks out adults and bullies. And I'll give it away free to all kids who suffer at their hands.

I've even got a name for it: Banger.

Jim Eldridge is a Superhero in disguise as an Ordinary Writer Who Lives In Cumbria. Unfortunately his fear of heights means he doesn't leap over tall buildings or fly. Also, because he can't tie his shoelaces properly or manage zips, his Supercostume is held together with Velcro, which sometimes comes apart when it's wet, so he can't go out in the rain.

When he is not out Saving the Planet, Jim writes books and television programmes such as 'The Ghost Hunter' and 'Julia Jekyll and Harriet Hyde'.

DISGUSTING DAVE

AND THE
FLESH-EATING MAGGOTS

Dave has a new interest, besides snot and sick
and other fascinating aspects of the human body.
Now he's finding out about maggots that hatch in
your flesh and then eat their way out.
It's enough to make his squeamish Aunt Dora
faint on the spot!

When some real-live
maggots arrive for Dave in
the post, his life becomes
truly complicated. Can he
keep the squirmy
wormlets under control
before they chomp their
way through the whole
neighbourhood?

978-1-444-90011-8